"What a difference twenty-four hours can make."

He faced the woman who was now beside him.

"Last night at this time," Carly explained, "I was slamming the door on you."

"Oh, that. Well, this hasn't been what I'd call an average day."

"Me either. But I appreciate everything you did for us today, Andrew."

He dared to meet her gaze. "I didn't do much."

"You were there for me when I needed you." She went to him, rose up on her toes and hugged him. "Thank you." Her words were a whisper on his ear, soft and warm. And he felt his world shift.

Then she turned for the door. "Good night."

Stunned, he managed to eke out, "Night," before she disappeaered into the house.

He stood there, waiting to breathe. Carly stirred something in him that he hadn't felt…well, since they were a couple.

That was not good. Because despite today's events, there was still the issue of his grandmother's house. And that was a battle he intended to win.

It took **Mindy Obenhaus** forty years to figure out what she wanted to do when she grew up. But once God called her to write, she never looked back. She's passionate about touching readers with biblical truths in an entertaining, and sometimes adventurous, manner. Mindy lives in Texas with her husband and kids. When she's not writing, she enjoys cooking and spending time with her grandchildren. Find more at mindyobenhaus.com.

Books by Mindy Obenhaus

Love Inspired

Rocky Mountain Heroes

Their Ranch Reunion

The Doctor's Family Reunion
Rescuing the Texan's Heart
A Father's Second Chance
Falling for the Hometown Hero

Their Ranch Reunion

Mindy Obenhaus

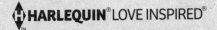

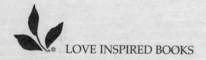

LOVE INSPIRED BOOKS

Recycling programs
for this product may
not exist in your area.

ISBN-13: 978-0-373-62295-5

Their Ranch Reunion

Copyright © 2017 by Melinda Obenhaus

www.Harlequin.com

Printed in U.S.A.

open just enough to insert her key into the lock of the old wooden door. Then, thanks to the ongoing hammering sound, she slipped inside undetected.

The seventies-era kitchen, complete with avocado-green appliances and gold countertops, looked the same as it had every other time she'd been there in recent weeks. Pathetic. She still couldn't understand why Livie would do such a horrendous thing to this charming house. Carly could hardly wait to get rid of that ugly old stuff and replace it with a look that was truer to the home's original character.

Bang. Bang. Bang.

Carly jumped, sending her renovation ideas flying out the window. At least until she took care of whoever was in the parlor.

Raising the bat, she tiptoed into the short hallway, past the closet, until she could see who was making that racket.

She peered around the corner, nearly coming unglued when she spotted the male figure crouched beside the wall on the other side of the kitchen, using a hammer and a crowbar to remove the original trim moldings.

She slammed the tip of the bat onto the worn wooden floor with a crash. "*What* are you doing to my house?"

The man jumped. Jerking his head in her direction, he hustled to his feet until he towered over her.

Carly gasped. *What is he doing here?*

Eyes wide, she simply gaped. The perpetrator wasn't just any man. Instead, Andrew Stephens, Livie's grandson, stood before her, looking none too pleased.

Heat started in her belly, quickly rising to her cheeks. Though it had been nearly twenty years since they'd dated and she'd seen him a few times since, her mind failed to recall that the boy she once knew so well was now a man. A very tall, muscular man with thick, dark brown hair, penetrating brown eyes and a stubble beard that gave him a slightly dangerous, albeit very appealing, look.

His surprise morphed into irritation. "Your house?"

She struggled for composure, jutting her chin in the air while trying to ignore the scent of raw masculinity. "You heard me." Aware she wasn't acknowledging the complete truth, her courage suddenly waned. "Well, half of it anyway."

Andrew eyed her bat. "I'm not sure where you're getting your information, Carly, but this house belongs to me." Shifting his tools from one hand to the other, he moved closer. "And I have a copy of my grandmother's will that proves it."

Oh, so he thought he could intimidate her, did he? Not to mention call her a liar?

She laid one hand over the other atop the bat. "That's odd. Because I received a letter from Livie's lawyer, along with a copy of her will, and it stated that the house passes equally to both you and me." And while her plan was to offer to buy out his half, this probably wasn't the best time to bring that up.

He cocked his head, his expression softening a notch. "Are you okay? You haven't hit your head or something, have you?"

She sucked in a breath, indignation twisting her gut. Wasn't it enough that he'd broken her young heart? Now he thought she was crazy. Well, she'd show him.

Resting the bat on her shoulder, she whirled and started for the back door.

"Where are you going?"

"I'll be *right* back." She stormed out the door and marched over to her house, kicking at a dwindling pile of snow along the way. Did he really think she was going to

Forget the former things;
do not dwell on the past. See, I am doing a
new thing! Now it springs up; do you not
perceive it? I am making a way in the
wilderness and streams in the wasteland.
—*Isaiah* 43:18–19

For Your glory, Lord.

Acknowledgments

A big thank-you to Captain Glen Vincent, Village Fire Department, for your twenty-nine years of service as a firefighter and for your willingness to share your knowledge.

Thanks to Wendy Jilek at Colorado Kitchen and Bath Design, Montrose, Colorado, for your input on the kitchen-design process.

Much appreciation to Catrina at ServePro of Montrose and Telluride.

And I couldn't have done any of this without the love and support of my incredible husband. Thank you for being my rock.

Chapter One

If she had to look at one more spreadsheet, she'd go batty.

Overdue for a break, Carly Wagner pushed away from her laptop at the oak kitchen table, poured another cup of tea and wandered into the parlor of her Victorian home. The late morning sun filtered through the windows, bathing the somewhat formal though still cozy room in warmth. Taking a sip of her Cream Earl Grey, she glimpsed the photo of her great-grandmother on the mantel and smiled. Granger House was more than just her home. The bed-and-breakfast was a way of life.

She let go a sigh. If only she didn't have to keep taking in these bookkeeping jobs to help build up her savings. But if she hoped to send her daughter, Megan, to college one day…

She was just about to sit in the powder-blue accent chair when something outside caught her attention. Easing toward the side window, she noticed a vehicle in the driveway next door. She fingered the lace curtain aside and peered through the antique glass pane.

That truck did not belong there.

Her neighbor, Olivia Monroe, Livie to everyone who knew her, had been dead for six months. Since then, no one had set foot in that house without Carly's knowledge. Until now.

Narrowing her gaze on the ginormous black F-350, curiosity mingled with concern. After all, Livie's house now belonged to her. Well, maybe not completely, but Lord willing, it would, just as soon as she convinced Livie's grandson, Andrew, to sell her his half. That is, once she finally mustered the courage to call her old high school boyfriend. Then she would finally be able to act on her dream of expanding Granger House Inn and kiss bookkeeping goodbye.

Allowing the curtain to fall back into place, she paced from the wooden floor to the large Persian rug in the center of the room and back again. What should she do? She hated to bother the police. Not that they had much to do in a quiet town like Ouray, Colorado. Then again, if it was nothing, she'd look like the nosy neighbor who worried over everything.

No, she needed to do a little investigation before calling the cops.

She headed back into the kitchen, depositing her cup on the butcher-block island before grabbing her trusty Louisville Slugger on her way out the back door. The cool air sent a shiver down her spine. At least, that's what she told herself. Realistically, it was rather mild for the second day of March. Perhaps the sun would help rid them of what remained of their most recent snowfall.

Making herself as small as possible, she crept across the drive and around the back of Livie's folk Victorian. Banging echoed from inside. Or was it her own heart slamming against her rib cage?

With Livie's house key clenched in her sweaty palm, Carly drew in a bolstering breath and continued a few more feet. She soundlessly eased the metal storm door let him plead ignorance when she had proof? That house was half hers and she refused to be bullied.

Once inside Granger House, Carly went straight to her bedroom, opened the small safe she kept tucked in the corner and pulled out the large manila envelope. Let Andrew argue with this.

Leaving her bat in her kitchen for fear she might actually be tempted to use it, she again made her way next door, irritation nipping at her heels. She would not let Andrew stand between her and her dream.

When she entered this time, he was in the kitchen, arms crossed, leaning against the peninsula that separated the eating space from the food-prep space, looking better than an ex-boyfriend should.

She removed the papers from the envelope and handed them to him. "Page three, last paragraph."

She watched as he read, noting the lines carved deeply into his brow. So serious. Intense. And while he had never been the carefree type, it appeared the big city might have robbed him of whatever joy remained.

When he glanced her way, she quickly lowered her gaze. Just because she hadn't seen him in forever didn't give her the right to stare. No matter how intriguing the sight.

"I don't get it." He flipped back to the front page. "This will was drawn up only a year and a half ago." He looked at her now. "The one I have is at least five years old. Meaning this—" he wiggled the papers— "supersedes that."

Carly rested her backside against the wood veneer table, her fingers gripping the edge. "So, are you saying you *didn't* receive a letter from your grandmother's lawyer?"

He shook his head. "Not that I'm aware of."

This was her chance to make her move. Before she chickened out. "I'm sorry to hear that. However—" she shoved away from the table "—we can take care of this quite easily." She lifted her chin. "I'd like to buy out your half. I've been looking for a way to expand my bed-and-breakfast, and this house is the perfect solution. Besides, you're never in Ouray—"

"I love this house. Always have. You know that."

While she knew that Andrew the boy had loved the house, she could count the times Andrew the man had set foot in Ouray since moving to Denver right after graduation. A move that was supposed to be the beginning of their future together. Instead, it had torn them apart.

Refusing to let the painful memories get the best of her, she crossed her arms over her chest. "Until today, when was the last time you were in this house?"

"After my grandmother's funeral."

"And the time before that?" She awaited a response.

After a long moment, he shoved the papers back at her. "This house has been in my family for four generations. And I'm not about to let that change anytime soon. Even for you."

Andrew hadn't been this bowled over since Crawford Construction, one of Denver's largest commercial builders, offered to buy out his company, Pinnacle Construction. Even then, he hadn't been totally unaware. He'd heard rumors. But this revelation about his grandmother's house took him completely by surprise.

There was no way he was going to sell Carly half of the house that rightfully belonged to him. There had to be some mistake. He hadn't even been notified of the change to Grandma's will.

Watching out the kitchen window as Carly made her way back to Granger House, her blond curls bouncing with each determined step, he could think of only two explanations. His grandmother was crazy, or Carly had somehow coerced her into changing her will, giving his high school sweetheart half of the house that had been promised to him from the time he was a boy.

He continued his scrutiny, chuckling at the memory of Carly holding that baseball bat. Coming into the house, not knowing who was inside, took a lot of guts. Apparently the shy girl he'd once known no longer existed. Then again, that was a long time ago. She'd since become a wife, a mother, a widow… Not to mention one of the most beautiful women he'd ever seen.

Shaking off the unwanted observation, he waited for her to disappear inside her house before digging the keys out of his jeans pocket and heading out the door. He had to get to the bottom of this and fast. For months, he'd been looking forward to updating this old home to use as a rental property. Now, as he awaited the closing on his next business venture, he had eight weeks to do just that.

He climbed into his truck and fired up the diesel engine, daring a glance toward Granger House. With its sea foam green paint, intricate millwork and expansive front porch, the historic Victorian home looked much the way it would have when it was first built nearly one hundred twenty years ago. Today's guests must feel as though they're stepping back in time.

His gaze drifted to the swing at the far end of the porch. Back when he and Carly were dating, they spent many an evening there, holding hands, talking about their plans for the future. Plans he once thought would include her.

But that was then. This was now.

He threw the truck into gear and set off for his grandmother's lawyer's office, only to discover the man was out of town for the week. Frustration burrowed deeper.

He didn't know what to do. Perhaps his father would have some insight.

Andrew's shoulders slumped. Seeing his father meant a trip to the ranch. Something he hadn't planned to do just yet.

If he wanted answers, though, it was his only option.

He maneuvered his truck onto Main Street, past the rows of colorful historic buildings, to continue north of town, beyond the walls of red sandstone, on to the open range. A few minutes later, he passed under the arched metal sign that read Abundant Blessings Ranch. Why his parents had named the place that, he'd never understand. Their lives were far from blessed, working their fingers to the bone with little to nothing to show for it.

He'd never live like that again.

Bumping up the gravel drive, he eyed the snow-capped mountains that stretched across the far edge of the property, beyond the river where they used to fish and swim.

A couple of horses watched him from the corral as he passed the stable. Red with white trim, it was the newest building on Stephens' land. Apparently the trail rides his father and oldest brother Noah offered during the summer months had been successful. That, in addition to the riding lessons Noah taught, had likely funded the structure.

The old barn, however, was another story. Closer to the house, the rustic wooden outbuilding had seen better days. The roof sagged, the pens on the outside were missing most of their slats and the ancient shingles were in sore need of replacing. Better yet, someone should just bulldoze the thing and start fresh.

A task he could easily take care of once they were well into spring. But he'd be back in Denver by then, the proud owner of Magnum Custom Home Builders.

He pulled alongside his father's beat-up dually, killed

the engine and stepped outside to survey the single-story ranch house.

Though the sun was warm, a chill sifted through him. He wouldn't have believed it possible, but the place looked even worse than it had six months ago when he was here for his grandmother's funeral. The cedar siding was the darkest he'd ever seen it. The house, along with the large wooden deck that swept across one side, could use a good power-washing. Not that Dad, Noah or his younger brother, Jude, had the time. Before the cancer took its toll, the house had always been Mama's domain. And with five sons eager to please her, she was never at a loss for help.

The back door opened then, and Clint Stephens stepped outside, clad in his usual Wrangler jeans and chambray work shirt. "I thought I heard an engine out here." Smiling, his father started toward the three short steps separating him from Andrew, the heels of his well-worn cowboy boots thudding against the wood.

"How's it going, Dad?"

"It goes." His father cocked his graying head and peered down at him. "You no longer feel the need to tell your old man when you're coming back to Ouray?"

Andrew pushed the mounting guilt aside. "Maybe I wanted to surprise you." Hands shoved in his pockets, he perched his own booted foot on the bottom step. "I was planning to do some work on Grandma's house, but it seems she changed her will. You wouldn't happen to know anything about that, would you?"

"I do. I'm kinda surprised you don't, though."

"Why?"

"Didn't you get a copy of the new one?"

"No, sir."

"Hmm…" His father rubbed the gray stubble lining his jaw. "Guess we'd better have a talk, then." He turned back toward the house. "I just put on a fresh pot of coffee. Care to join me?"

After toeing out of their boots in the mudroom, they continued into the family room. Though the mottled brown carpet Andrew remembered from his childhood had been replaced with wood laminate flooring, the room still looked much the same with its oversize furniture and wood-burning stove.

He eyed the large Oriental rug in the middle of the room. Mama had been so tickled when he'd given it to her the Christmas after the new flooring had been put in. Said the rich colors made her simple house feel more grand.

While his father moved into the kitchen that was more like an extension of the family room, or vice versa, Andrew stood frozen, held captive by the wall of framed photos at the end of the room. Baby pictures of him and his brothers. Graduation photos. Milestones and achievements. There had never been a prouder mama than Mona Stephens.

Guilt nearly strangled him. He hadn't even had the respect to be here when she died.

"You still take it black?"

Turning, Andrew cleared his throat before addressing his father. "Just like you taught me."

The corners of Dad's mouth twitched. "There's some roast beef in the fridge." He motioned with a nod. "Help yourself if you're hungry."

Considering Andrew hadn't eaten anything since he pulled out of Denver well before sunup…

He spread mayonnaise on a slice of white bread, recalling his last visit before his mother's death. Despite chemo treatments, she still had his favorite foods waiting for him. From homemade apple pie to beef stroganoff, the most incredible aromas filled the house.

He glanced around the dated L-shaped kitchen. This old ranch house would never again smell so good.

"If you didn't get a copy of the new will, how'd you find out about the change?" Dad eased into one of the high-backed chairs at the old wooden table near the wall.

"Carly paid me an unexpected visit." He picked up his sandwich and joined the old man. "So, what gives? Grandma promised her house to me. I have a copy of her will that proves it. Why'd she make the change?"

Dad set his stained mug inscribed with #1 Dad atop the table. "Carly meant a lot to Livie. She was a friend, a caretaker and the granddaughter she never had."

"Okay, but Carly isn't family."

"Not by blood. But like I said, Livie thought of her as family. They were very good friends, you know."

"No. I didn't know." Andrew took a bite. Sounded like Carly went to great lengths to worm her way into his grandmother's life, all to expand her bed-and-breakfast.

"After Carly lost her husband, she and Livie grew even closer. Your grandmother understood what Carly was going through."

Something Carly probably used to her advantage.

"No one can understand the pain of a young widow better than someone who was also a young widow." Dad lifted his cup and took another sip of coffee. "That aside, your grandmother had her concerns that you might sell the place." His gaze settled on Andrew. "Making Carly half owner might have been her way of ensuring that the house remained with someone she loved."

"But I've always wanted that house. That's why Grandma left it to me in the first place." That and the fact that none of his brothers were interested. "I would never consider selling."

"You were in Denver, hardly ever came home."

Guilt wedged deeper. Even if he'd found the time to come back, he wasn't sure he could face the judgmental looks he was bound to receive from his brothers. As though he'd betrayed them for not getting here before Mama died.

"What are you planning to do with the house, anyway, son?"

His appetite waning, Andrew wrapped his suddenly cold fingers around the hot cup his father had given him. "Open up the bottom floor, add an extra bath, update the kitchen... I was hoping to have it ready by the high season to use as a rental."

"Sounds like quite an undertaking."

Andrew shrugged, still suspicious of the relationship between his grandmother and Carly. "You know, Carly mentioned something about wanting to expand Granger House Inn. You don't suppose she shared those plans with Grandma in hopes of getting her hands on that house, do you? I mean, it is right next door."

His father's brow furrowed. "It's possible she made mention of it. But Carly's not the scheming type. You know that."

Did he?

"Apparently she's pretty determined," Andrew said, "because she offered to buy my half of Grandma's house."

Lips pursed, Dad nodded in a matter-of-fact manner. "You gonna take her up on it?"

"No." Andrew shoved his sandwich aside. "What was Grandma thinking?"

Dad chuckled, lifting his cup. "Doesn't really matter, son. You and Carly are just going to have to find a way to work it out."

Chapter Two

"Yes, we do have an opening for Easter weekend." Sitting at her kitchen table that afternoon, Carly settled the phone between her ear and shoulder, grateful for the distraction. Her mind had been reeling ever since her encounter with Andrew.

She brought up the reservations page on her laptop. "The Hayden Room is available. It has a queen-size bed, a private bathroom and a spectacular view of Hayden Mountain."

"Oh, yes. I think I saw that one on your website." Excitement laced the female caller's tone. "It's beautiful."

Carly couldn't help smiling. Actually, all of their guest rooms were on the website. Something that had garnered Granger House many a booking. The problem she most often encountered, though, was when a group of people or a family required more space or multiple rooms she didn't have available. That was exactly where Livie's house would benefit her. Not only could she book the three rooms there individually but also market the entire house to those larger parties. Whatever the case, the addition of Livie's house would virtually double her income.

"I guarantee you won't be disappointed." She took hold of the phone. "Would you like to reserve it?"

"Yes, please. For Friday and Saturday night."

Ah, yes. There was nothing Carly loved more than a fully booked weekend. Especially this time of year when things tended to be a little sparse. Looked like she'd better get her breakfast menus planned. Though it was still a few weeks away, Easter weekend was extra special. There'd be ham to prepare, biscuits, scones...

She took the caller's information, hanging up as the kitchen timer went off.

Standing, she grabbed a pot holder and moved to the commercial-style range to retrieve a large baking sheet from the oven. Within seconds, her kitchen was filled with the aromas of cinnamon and vanilla.

She crossed the wide expanse of original hardwood and deposited the pan on the island. Until learning she'd inherited half of Livie's house, Carly had been saving to remodel the kitchen at Granger House. While the room was large, it had one of the worst layouts ever, with the stove by itself at one end of the room and the refrigerator clear over on the other. Not to mention the lack of counter space. But since she'd be using that money to buy out Andrew's half of Livie's house, she'd just have to live with it a while longer.

Too bad Andrew had to be so difficult. Okay, so the house had been in his family for generations. She'd give him that. But unless he was planning to move back to Ouray, what possible use could he have for it? The place would just sit there empty.

Nope, no matter how she looked at it, there was no way this co-owning thing was going to work, and she couldn't help wondering why Livie had set things up that way. Unless...

She picked up her spatula to remove the cookies, then stopped. Oh, say it wasn't so. Livie had never tried to play matchmaker for Andrew and her while she was alive. Why would she do it in death?

No, no. Carly refused to believe it.

Still shaking her head, she shoveled the cookies from the baking sheet to the cooling rack. Regardless of Livie's intentions, no matter what they might have been, Carly would simply have to figure out how to convince Andrew to sell her his half. She would not let him rob her of another dream. Not when this one was so close.

Back when she first took over Granger House from her parents seven years ago, she had grand ideas and had expressed an interest in expanding when the house on the opposite side of them came on the market. Her late husband, Dennis, had never been fond of the idea, though, so she'd tucked those dreams away. After his death two years later, she was too busy caring for Megan and simply trying to keep up to even think about anything other than what was absolutely necessary. But as Megan got older, Carly would occasionally revisit her daydreams. Still, with the other house no longer available, that's all they were.

Until Livie's death. Suddenly it was as though God had granted the desires of her heart in a way she never would have imagined. After all, just like Granger House, Livie's house was only a block off Main Street, affording guests easy access to just about everything in town. And the fact that a narrow drive was all that separated the two houses made it the perfect candidate for her expansion.

At least until Andrew showed up, thinking he was going to claim his inheritance.

She let go a sigh. How was she, a simple small-town girl who'd spent her entire life in Ouray, going to convince some bigwig businessman like Andrew? It wasn't as if their romantic history would score her any brownie points.

Her gaze drifted to the cookies. And plying him with food wasn't likely to do the job, either.

Lord, show me what I should do. Because right now, it looks as though Andrew and I are at an impasse.

The back door opened then, bringing a surge of cool air as nine-year-old Megan bounded inside.

"Mmm…cookies." Her daughter dropped her backpack on the wooden floor.

"You're just in time. They're fresh out of the oven."

Without bothering to take off her coat, Megan rushed over and grabbed one. "Yay, snickerdoodles!" She took a big bite.

Carly snagged her own cookie, pleased that her daughter appreciated her culinary skills. And running a bed-and-breakfast, she was almost always cooking something. If not directly for her guests, then she was trying out new recipes. Something her friends benefited from, making it a win-win for Carly. They gave her feedback and she didn't have to worry about her waistline. Well, not as much, anyway.

"How was school?"

With the cinnamon-coated treat sticking out of her mouth, Megan shrugged out of her coat. "Good." She dropped the puffy thing on a hook near the door before plopping into one of the Windsor-style chairs at the table to finish her snack. "Who's at Ms. Livie's house?"

Carly glanced out the window to see Andrew's big black truck once again in the driveway. With all the noise that thing made, she was surprised she hadn't heard him pull in.

Why was he back, anyway? After watching him leave

this morning, she'd hoped he'd decided to stay away until they reached an agreement.

"That would be her grandson, Andrew." She grabbed a glass from the cupboard and continued on to the refrigerator for the milk.

"Do I know him?" Megan's blue eyes followed Carly as she moved toward her daughter.

She set the glass, along with another cookie, in front of her. "He's the one who played cards with you, me and Livie a couple of years ago."

"When Ms. Livie's daughter died, right?"

"That's him." She ruffled Megan's straighter-than-straight strawberry blond hair, a trait she definitely didn't inherit from her mother. But after decades of fighting her natural curls, Carly had finally learned to embrace them. "You have a good memory."

"Why is he at Ms. Livie's house now, though?" Megan picked up the second cookie. "I thought she gave it to you."

Carly cringed. She'd had no business mentioning that to Megan until the estate had been settled. Yet in her excitement over the news all those months back, she'd blurted it out without thinking.

"She gave me half of it. And she gave Andrew the other half."

"Which half is yours?"

Carly puffed out a laugh. She could only imagine what was going through her daughter's nine-year-old mind. As if Carly and Andrew could just slap a piece of tape down the middle.

"Unfortunately, it's not quite that simple." And if she couldn't get Andrew to sell her his half, she'd be stuck taking in people's accounting books until Megan graduated college.

Megan stood, dusting the crumbs from her hands. "Can I go over there?"

"I don't think that's a very good idea right now." If ever. At least, not with Andrew there. Mr. Serious likely wouldn't tolerate kids.

Still, she couldn't help wondering what he was up to. Not after catching him removing baseboards this morning. Baseboards he'd better plan on putting back, because she wasn't about to stand by and let him strip the home of its character.

"On second thought, maybe we should go over there and say hi." And if their presence happened to remind him that she was keeping tabs on him, so be it.

Megan paused at the island, looking very serious. "We should take him some cookies."

Hand perched on her hip as she watched her daughter, Carly wasn't sure how she felt about the suggestion. However, it was Livie who'd always said you caught more flies with honey than with vinegar. And right about now, there was one big fly Carly was interested in catching.

"I think that's a terrific idea."

"Well, that's just great."

Andrew dropped his phone on the counter in his grandmother's kitchen. He'd been calling his attorney's cell all afternoon. When he finally decided to try the office, he learned that the man was in court and wouldn't be available until tomorrow.

He blew out a frustrated breath. This was not how he'd envisioned this day playing out.

Pushing away from the cabinet, he paced the ugly gold-and-brown vinyl floor while he waited for a pot of coffee to brew. He knew it was a long shot, but perhaps Ned could find a way to get Grandma's will overturned and the original reinstated. Then all of his problems would be solved.

You and Carly are just going to have to find a way to work it out.

Hmph. Dad always did look at things simplistically. The only thing simple about the dispute between him and Carly was the fact that they both wanted this house.

As the coffeemaker spewed out its last efforts, Andrew grabbed a mug from the cupboard. If it hadn't been for Carly, he could have had at least one wall taken down by now. Enough to give him an idea of how the house was going to look with an open concept. Instead, he was left with a whole lot of nothing to do.

Leaning against the counter, he took a sip. He'd loved his grandmother dearly, but leaving her house to both him and Carly had to be the craziest idea she'd had since she went white-water rafting down the Uncompahgre River at the age of eighty-three. Except for sharing a game of cards after his mother's funeral, he and Carly had barely spoken in seventeen years. Not since the day she turned down his marriage proposal and walked out of his life forever.

Relegating the unwanted memories to the darkest corner of his mind, he scanned the sorry-looking kitchen. While he wasn't about to give up on getting his grandmother's old will reinstated, he could still be proactive, just in case things didn't work out the way he hoped. Near as he could tell, there were only two ways out of this predicament. And since selling his half to Carly was out of the question, that left him with only one option—he'd have to buy out Carly's half of the house. Something that chafed him more than he cared to admit.

Aside from paying for something that was rightfully his to begin with, he'd have to come up with an offer better than hers. Sweeten the deal, so to speak, making it too good to refuse. Much like the company who'd just bought him out. And left him with a tidy chunk of change. Carly would be able to do whatever she liked with Granger House and leave this house—and him—alone.

"Hello, hello." As though he'd willed her to appear, Carly pushed open the back door, knocking as she came.

Try as he might, he couldn't ignore the fact that she was still one of the most gorgeous women he'd ever seen. The kind that could take your breath away with her natural beauty.

Her blond curls brushed across her shoulders as she held the door, allowing a young girl to enter first.

Her daughter had grown quite a bit since the last time he'd seen her. What was her name? Maggie? No, Megan.

"Hi." The girl smiled up at him with blue eyes reminiscent of her mother's and waved. In her other hand she held a small plate covered with plastic wrap. "We brought you cookies." She handed them to him.

So these were Carly's weapons of choice. Children and food. Ranked right up there with little old ladies.

His conscience mentally kicked his backside. Dad was right. Carly wasn't the type to try to steal his grandmother's house. However, that didn't mean he was simply going to hand it over.

While Megan wandered off as though she lived there, he set the plate on the counter and helped himself to a cookie. "Snickerdoodles. How did you know I was in need of a snack?" He took a bite.

The feisty blonde watched him suspiciously. "What brings you back here?"

He chased the first homemade treat he'd had in a long time with a swig of coffee. "I'm—"

"Uh-oh." Megan's voice echoed from the next room. "Somebody made a mess."

After a moment, Carly tore her gaze away from him and started into the front room.

Andrew set his cup on the counter and followed.

Rounding the corner into the home's only living space, he saw Megan pointing at the small stack of baseboards he'd begun to remove this morning. Before his plans were rerouted by Carly.

"I was doing a little work."

Carly lifted a brow. "I'm not sure what kind of work it was, but you need to put those back."

Irritation sparked. Who was she to start giving him orders?

"Whose is this?" Now on the other side of the room, Megan rocked back and forth in his grandmother's glider, pointing to the duffel he'd left by the front door. He wouldn't go so far as to call the kid nosy, but she was definitely curious. Not to mention observant.

"That would be mine." He turned to find Carly watching him.

Both brows were up in the air this time. "Planning to stay a while?"

This was ridiculous. He should not be interrogated in his own house. "As a matter of fact, I am. For several weeks. Which reminds me—" he crossed his arms over chest "—I think we need to set up a time to talk." Glancing at Megan, he lowered his voice. "Privately."

Mirroring his stance, Carly said, "I was thinking the same thing."

"At least we're in agreement about something."

"I'm going upstairs." A sigh accompanied Megan's announcement, quickly followed by the clomping of boots on the wooden steps.

Andrew knew just how she felt.

With Megan gone, Carly addressed him. "I'm curious.

Before you learned that you were not the sole owner of this house, what were your intentions for it? I mean, were you planning to move in?"

"Temporarily, yes. I'm going to update the place and use it for rental income."

Seemingly confused, she said, "Where will you be?"

"Denver, of course."

Lines appeared on her forehead. "Let me get this straight." She perched both hands on her hips. "You don't want me to use Livie's house for my bed-and-breakfast, yet you want to turn it into rental property?"

"In a nutshell, yes."

"Why not just rent your half to me?"

It wasn't that he didn't like Carly. He wasn't purposely trying to thwart her plans. But this house was supposed to be his and his alone.

He dared a step closer. "Because, should I come back to Ouray, I want to be able to stay here. *Without* having to share it with someone else."

She shook her head. "So you'd rather pay me half of the rent money you get? That makes no sense."

"Pay you? Why would I—?"

"Mommy?" Megan hopped down the stairs, one loud thud at a time.

Carly seemed to compose herself before shifting her attention to her daughter. "What is it, sweetie?"

The girl tugged on Carly's sleeve, urging her closer, then cupped a hand over her mother's ear. "We should invite him for dinner." For all her implied secrecy, Megan had failed to lower her voice.

A look that could only be described as sheer horror flitted across Carly's face. Her eyes widened. "Oh, I'm sure Andrew already has plans for—"

"Nope. No plans at all." Fully aware of her discomfort, he simply shook his head, awaiting her response.

Clearing her throat, Carly straightened, looking none too happy. "In that case, would you care to join us for dinner?" She practically ground out the words.

He couldn't help smiling. "Sure. Why not?"

Watching them leave a short time later, he knew good and well that Carly was no more excited about having him for dinner than he was about sharing his grandmother's house. But as Grandma was fond of saying, it is what it is.

Who knew? Maybe they'd have an opportunity to talk. And if all went well, by the time this evening was over, Grandma's house would belong to him and him alone.

Chapter Three

Carly removed the meat loaf from the oven and put in the apple pie she'd tossed together at the last minute. Throw in some mashed potatoes and green beans and it was comfort food all the way. She'd need all the comfort she could get if she hoped to make it through an evening with the man who had once been able to read her every thought.

Using a pot holder, she picked up the pan of meat and headed for the island. *Nope. No plans at all.* She all but flung the pan on the counter, sending spatters of tomato sauce across the butcher-block top.

She grabbed a rag and wiped up the mess, knowing good and well that Andrew was simply trying to get her goat. And enjoying every minute of it, no doubt. Just like he did back in high school. Only she was no longer the timid girl who was afraid to stand up for herself.

After throwing the rag into the sink, she returned to the stove to check the potatoes. Fork in hand, she lifted the lid on the large pot.

It irked her that Andrew was planning to use Livie's house as a rental. Why wouldn't he just let— Wait a minute.

Steam billowed in front of her.

She was half owner. That meant she had a say in what went on next door. He couldn't use it as a rental without her permission.

Smiling, she poked at the vegetables. Yep, they were done.

She replaced the lid and carried the pot to the sink. This whole dispute would be over if Andrew would simply agree to sell. Unfortunately, for as eager as she was to discuss purchasing his half of the house so she could move forward with her expansion plans, she wasn't at liberty to talk business with Megan in the room. Which meant this whole evening was a waste of time.

That is, unless her idea of plying Andrew with food actually worked.

Holding the lid slightly off-center so as not to lose any of the potatoes, she drained the water from the pot. Maybe he'd be in such a state of gastronomic euphoria by the end of this evening that it would be impossible for him to say no when she again extended her offer.

Dream on, girl.

"Can I help?" Megan emerged from the adjoining family room at the back of the house, directly off the kitchen. Carly's parents had built the addition when she was young as a private space for the family. Now Carly appreciated it more than ever, because it allowed her to keep an eye on her daughter while she worked in the kitchen.

"Of course you can. Care to set the table?"

"Okay."

Carly opened the cupboard to grab the plates.

"Not those plates, Mommy."

"What?" She glanced down at her daughter.

"We need the guest plates." Meaning the china she used for the bed-and-breakfast. And this time of year, guests were predominantly limited to weekends.

"Sweetie, we don't use those for regular meals."

"This isn't a regular meal. Mr. Andrew is company, so we need to eat in the dining room with the pretty dishes."

Oh, to be a child again, when everything was so simple. *Lord, help me make it through tonight.*

"Okay. Let me get them for you."

They moved around the corner into the dining room, and Carly retrieved the dishes from atop her grandmother's antique sideboard. Meat loaf on china. That'd be a first.

Leaving Megan in charge of the table, Carly returned to the kitchen to mash the potatoes. She pulled the butter and cream from the large stainless steel refrigerator.

"Which side do the forks go on?"

Closing the refrigerator door, Carly grinned, recalling how she used to help her mother and wondering if Megan would one day take over Granger House Inn. If so, she'd be the third generation to run the B and B. Not that she was in any hurry for her daughter to grow up. Carly was already lamenting Megan's occasional usage of Mom instead of Mommy.

"On the left."

A knock on the back door nearly had Carly dropping the dairy products she still held.

Megan must have heard it, too, because she raced past Carly and threw open the door.

Carly deposited the butter and cream on the counter and hurried behind her daughter. "Young lady, what have I told you about looking to see who it is before you open the door?" Not that there was much to worry about in Ouray. Still, a mother could never be too cautious in this day and age.

"Sorry."

"Evening, ladies." A smiling Andrew stepped inside,

looking far too appealing. His hair was damp, and he smelled freshly showered.

Closing the door behind him, Carly eyed her flour-speckled jeans. Clearly he'd done more primping than she had. An observation that had her as curious as it did bothered.

"Welcome to our home." Megan swept her arm through the air in a flourish.

"Thank you for inviting me." He stooped to her daughter's level. "This is for you." He handed her a small brown paper gift bag with white tissue sticking out the top.

Megan's eyes were wide. "For me?"

"Yep. And this one—" straightening, he turned his attention to Carly "—is for your mother."

Carly's heart tripped as she accepted the package. A hostess gift had been unexpected, but the fact that he'd thought of both of them had her reevaluating their guest. At least momentarily.

"Th-thank you."

"Can I open it?" Megan looked as if she was about to explode with anticipation.

"Of course. What are you waiting for?" Andrew looked like a kid himself as he watched Megan pull out the tissue, followed by a small rectangular box. "My own cards!"

"Did my grandmother ever teach you how to play Hearts?"

"I don't think so." Megan eyed him seriously.

"Looks like I'll have to carry on the tradition, then. Perhaps we can play a game after dinner."

"Okay." Megan excitedly removed the plastic wrapping. "I can practice shuffling now, though, can't I?"

"You sure can." Andrew looked at Carly again. "You can open yours, too."

Her stomach did a little flip-flop as she removed the

tissue and pulled out a small box from Mouse's Chocolates. "Ooo…"

"I hope you like truffles."

She lifted a shoulder. "No, not really."

His smile evaporated and, for just a moment, she felt bad for messing with him. Then again, after the way he'd coerced her into this dinner invitation, why should she care?

"Oh, I'm sorry. I thought most women—"

"I love them."

The corners of his mouth slowly lifted as he wagged a finger her way. "You had me going for a second."

Looking up, she sent him a mischievous grin. "Good."

She moved back toward the island, glad she had potatoes to keep her busy for a few minutes. Was it her imagination or did Andrew's brown eyes seem a touch lighter tonight? Like coffee with a splash of cream. Maybe it was the blue-gray mix in his flannel shirt. Whatever the case, it might be best if Megan kept him occupied for a while.

When they sat down to dinner a short time later, Andrew surveyed the table. "This is quite the spread." His gaze settled on Carly. "I wasn't expecting you to go to all this trouble."

Again, her insides betrayed her, quivering at his praise. "No trouble."

"Yeah. My mommy cooks like this *all* the time."

Suspecting her daughter was attempting a little matchmaking, Carly added, "Not all the time. And we rarely eat in the dining room."

He glanced about. "That's a shame. This is a nice room."

"Oh, it gets plenty of use with the bed-and-breakfast." She eyed her daughter across the table. "Shall we pray?"

After dinner, Andrew followed through with his promise and taught Megan Livie's favorite card game while

Carly cleaned up the kitchen. Not only was she surprised by his patience with Megan and the gentle way he encouraged her, she greatly appreciated it. While Dennis had been a good father, he always seemed to have more time for his work than he did for his family. A fact that had Carly practicing the art of overcompensation long before his death.

With the dishes done, Carly joined them in the dining room.

She smoothed a hand across her daughter's back. "I hate to put the kibosh on your fun, but tomorrow is a school day."

"But I'm beating him. Please, can we finish this game?"

As much as Carly wanted to resist, to tell Megan it was time for Andrew to leave, she didn't have the heart. "Go ahead."

Fifteen minutes later, with her first win under her belt and promises of a rematch, a happy Megan scurried off to get ready for bed.

Andrew pushed his chair in as he stood. "Think we could talk for a minute?"

"Um…" Carly's body tensed. While she had planned to reissue her offer to purchase his half of Livie's house, she wasn't sure she had the energy tonight. Then again, maybe he'd had a change of heart and was willing to accept her offer. "Okay. Let's go out front."

He followed her through the living room, past the carved wooden staircase and Victorian-era parlor chairs. "You've got a bright kid there. She's a fast learner."

Carly tugged open the heavy oak and leaded glass door. "I've always thought so."

Outside, the chilly evening air had her drawing her bulky beige cardigan around her. Moving to the porch swing, she sat down and stared out over the street. Once upon a time, she used to dream of finding someone who would sit with her and hold her hand while they talked about their day, the way her parents always had. Like she and Andrew used to do. And Dennis was too busy to do.

Now she knew better than to dream.

To her surprise, though, Andrew joined her on the swing. Close enough that she could feel the warmth emanating from his body.

"This has been a full day," he said.

If she thought her mind was muddled before he sat down… "Yes, it has." And she could hardly wait for it to be over.

He stretched his arm across the back of the swing, his long legs setting them into motion as he surveyed the neighborhood without saying a word.

For a split second, she wondered what he would do if she were to lean into him and rest her head on his shoulder. Would he wrap his arm around her and hold her close, the way he used to? Or would he push her away?

Feeling the cold seep into her bones, she pushed to her feet. "What was it you wanted to talk about?"

He hesitated a moment before joining her. Took in a deep breath. "I'm willing to pay you the full value of the house for your half."

Her jaw dropped. "Do you have any idea how much property values have risen around here?"

He shrugged. "I can afford it."

His words sparked a fire in her belly. He hadn't changed a bit. With Andrew, everything was about money. Making it, having it… Just like her late husband had been.

Well, he'd sorely underestimated her.

"I don't care if you offer me a million dollars. There are some things that just can't be bought. Including me."

Refusing to listen to another word, she stormed into the house and slammed the door behind her.

By noon the next day, Andrew was at his wit's end. Carly's adamant refusal last night, coupled with his former admin assistant's acknowledgment that a certified letter from Ouray had indeed come for him a few months back and was left on his desk, had him more confused than ever.

Tucked in a corner booth at Granny's Kitchen, a local diner he remembered as The Miner's Cafe, he listened to the din of the early lunch crowd and pondered what remained of his burger and fries. One would think he'd be used to Carly's rejection by now. At least last night's dismissal hadn't stung as much as when she'd refused to marry him.

He sighed, dipped a french fry into some ketchup and popped it in his mouth. Seventeen years later, he still wasn't sure what had gone wrong. But last night revealed something he hadn't expected. Despite everything, Carly still held a very special place in his heart. Simply being near her stirred up what-ifs and could-have-beens.

Rather absurd, if you asked him. They didn't even know each other anymore. Besides, he was headed back to Denver just as soon as he finished Grandma's house. And he knew all too well how Carly felt about the big city.

His phone vibrated in his pocket. He wiped his hands and slid out the device, happy to see his attorney's name on the screen.

He pressed the phone against his ear. "Hey, Ned."

"Judging from all the missed calls I have from you, I'm guessing you're eager to talk to me."

"Yes." He straightened in the wooden bench. "I was beginning to think you were avoiding me."

Ned laughed. "Sorry, buddy. I didn't think you'd be in

need of my services so soon. Don't tell me you're bored
with Ouray already."

Surprisingly, Ouray had been anything but boring this
time around.

"No, but I do have a problem." He pushed his plate aside
and proceeded to explain the change to his grandmother's
will. "Is there any way I can get this will revoked and the
original reinstated?" He reached for another fry, awaiting
his lawyer's response.

"Was your grandmother of sound mind? Did she have
dementia or anything?"

"Not that I'm aware of." Though given her decision to
split the ownership of the house, he was beginning to wonder. If it had been one of his brothers, he could understand
it. But Carly wasn't family.

"Then it's highly unlikely you'd be able to get it overturned."

Andrew wadded his napkin, tossed it on the high-gloss
wooden tabletop and raked a hand through his hair. He'd
anticipated as much. Still…

"Can I get you anything else?" Beside him, the waitress smiled down at him.

"One minute, Ned." He eyed the unquestionably pregnant blonde. "I'm good, thank you."

She slid him his check. "My name is Celeste if you
need anything else. Otherwise, you can pay at the register on your way out."

"Good deal. Thank you." He again set the phone to his
ear. "Sorry about that." He grabbed the ticket as he slipped
out of the booth. "So, what are my options?"

"You could—"

The town's emergency siren shrieked to life just then,
making it impossible for Andrew to hear anything. "Hold
on again, Ned." He stepped up to the register and paid

his tab as the high-pitched wail of fire trucks added to the discord.

When the madness finally settled, he stepped outside and resumed his call. "Okay, let's try this again." The cool midday air had him zipping up his jacket.

"And here I thought Ouray was just a sleepy little town."

Andrew looked up and down the historic Main Street. "Apparently not today."

Ned chuckled. "As far as options, you could offer to buy out the other person's half."

Crossing the street, Andrew let go a sigh. "Already did."

"And?"

"She slammed the door in my face." A quick glance heavenward had him noticing the plumes of thick, black smoke billowing into the air a few blocks away. Pretty significant fire, if you asked him. And fairly close to his grandmother's house.

A wave of unease rolled through him. "Uh, Ned, I'm gonna have to call you back."

He shoved the phone in his pocket, quickening his pace until he reached the corner. When he did, he peered to his right.

Dread pulsed through his veins as every nerve ending went on high alert. The fire trucks were in front of his grandmother's house.

He broke into a run. One block. Adrenaline urged him forward. Two blocks.

"Oh, no." Heart sinking, he came to a halt.

Across the street, smoke rolled from the back of Granger House Inn. Flames danced from the kitchen's side window, lapping at the sea foam paint, threatening the historic dentil moldings and clapboard siding.

One of the firemen barked orders, orchestrating the

chaos, while others flanked the corner of the house, their hoses aimed inside.

But where was Carly?

"Andrew!"

He jerked his head in the direction of his brother Jude's voice.

A police officer for the city of Ouray, his younger brother vehemently motioned him across the street.

Andrew hurried toward him.

"We need you to move your truck out of Grandma's drive."

"Sure thing." He tugged the keys from his pocket and threw himself into the vehicle, the smell of smoke nearly choking him.

As he backed into the street, he spotted Carly's SUV in front of her house. Where was she? Was she safe? Could she have been trapped inside? Oh, God. Please, no.

He quickly parked on the next block before rushing back.

People had gathered on the opposite side of the street, watching the horror unfold.

He scanned the faces, looking for Carly. She had to be here somewhere.

He again eyed the flames, feeling helpless. Sweat beaded his brow as panic surged through his body. *God, she has to be all right.*

Spotting Jude in the middle of the street, Andrew jogged toward him. "Where's Carly?"

"In the ambulance."

Ambulance?

He ran past the cluster of onlookers to the emergency vehicle parked a few houses down.

Drawing closer, he finally saw her, standing near the

rear bumper, attempting to pull off the oxygen mask while the female EMT fought to keep it over her face.

Andrew had never been so glad to see someone.

He slowed his pace as Carly ultimately ripped the mask from her face. "I don't need this." She coughed. "That's my house." More coughing. "I need to—"

Andrew stepped in front of her then. "You *need* to let the firemen do their job. And you *need* to get some good air into your lungs." He pulled the mask from her hand, noting the resignation in her blue eyes as she looked up at him, her bottom lip quivering. "At least for a little bit."

The fact that she didn't resist when he slipped the respirator over her head still surprised him. But when he reached for her hand, she quickly yanked it away.

He groaned. Stupid move. Who was he to try to comfort her?

Only then did he notice the way she cradled her hand, holding it against her torso. The redness. She'd been burned.

"I think we'd better get you into the ambulance."

She shook her head. "I want to see what's happening." The words were muffled through the plastic mask.

Andrew eyed the male and female EMTs. "Can she sit here while you look her over?" He gestured to the rear bumper.

They nodded.

He looked at Carly. "You promise to let them do what they need to do?"

A cough-filled moment ticked by before she finally agreed.

The female EMT checked Carly's vital signs as the man went to work on her hand. All the while, Carly's tearful gaze remained riveted on Granger House.

Andrew could only imagine the flurry of emotions

threatening to swallow her at any moment. The uncertainty, the grief… He wished he could make it all go away.

He sat down beside her as the man wrapped her hand in gauze. "What happened there?" Andrew pointed to the injury.

"I had gone to the bank." She coughed. "When I got back—" looking up, she blinked repeatedly "—I opened the back door and the…flames were everywhere."

His eyes momentarily drifted closed. Thank God she was okay.

Unable to stop himself, he slipped an arm around her shoulders and pulled her close. Despite wearing a jacket, her whole body shook.

Returning his attention to the house, he saw that the smoke had started to turn white, a sign that the fire was almost out. However, there was no telling what kind of damage it had left in its wake. Granger House was more than Carly's home. It was her livelihood. Without it—

As if she'd read his thoughts, Carly lifted her head, her eyes swimming with tears. "What am I going to do?"

Chapter Four

How could this have happened?

Carly stood beside the towering conifer in front of Livie's house a couple of hours later, her arms wrapped tightly around her middle. Staring at Granger House, she felt as though she were fighting to keep herself together. In only a short time, the fire had ravaged her majestic old home, leaving it scarred and disheveled.

At the back of the house, where the kitchen was located, soot trailed up the once beautiful sea foam green siding, leaving it blackened and ugly. Windows were missing and, as she strained to look inside, all she could see was black.

She breathed in deeply through her nose, trying to quell the nausea that refused to go away. If only they would let her go inside. Perhaps she'd find out things weren't as bad as they seemed.

The loud rumble of the fire engine filled her ears as firemen traipsed back and forth, returning hoses to their trucks. Carly eyed her gauze-wrapped hand. At least it didn't sting anymore. The smell of smoke would be forever seared into her memory, though. Not to mention the heat of those flames.

Tilting her head toward the cloud-dotted sky, she

blinked back tears. Save for a few years, she'd spent her entire life at Granger House. It was more than her home… it was family. An integral part of her heritage. Now she could only pray that the whole thing wasn't a loss. Even insurance couldn't replace that.

But what if it was a total loss? What would she do then?

"Can I get you anything? Are you warm enough?" The feel of Andrew's hand against the small of her back was a comfort she hadn't known in a long time. From the moment he appeared on the scene, Andrew had yet to leave her side. For once, she was grateful for his take-charge attitude. His presence was an unlikely calm in the midst of her storm.

"No, thank y—"

"Oh, my!"

Carly turned to see Rose Daniels, a family friend and owner of The Alps motel. Hand pressed against her chest, the white-haired woman studied the carnage. Beside her, Hillary Ward-Thompson, a former resident who'd recently returned, appeared every bit as aghast.

Carly knew exactly how they felt.

The dismay in Rose's blue eyes morphed into compassion as she shifted her attention to Carly, her arms held wide. "I came as soon as I heard." She hugged Carly with a strength that belied her eighty years. "You poor dear. Are you all right?"

She nodded against the older woman's shoulder, tears threatening again, but she refused to give in. She needed to stay strong.

After a long moment, Rose released her into Hillary's waiting embrace.

"I hate that this happened to you." Hillary stepped back, looking the epitome of chic with her perfectly styled short blond hair and silky tunic. Then again, Carly wouldn't expect anything less from the former globe-trotting exec.

"How can we help, dear?" Rose shoved her wrinkled hands into the pockets of her aqua Windbreaker. "Just tell us what you need."

"Besides food, that is," Hillary was quick to add. "Celeste has already talked to Blakely and Taryn. They're planning to bring you dinner." Her daughter, Celeste Purcell, owned Granny's Kitchen.

Carly hated that she'd added to their already hectic lives. "They don't have to—"

"Nonsense, darling." Hillary waved a hand through the air. "That's what people do in Ouray. You know that."

All too well. She'd been on the receiving end when Dennis died. Since then, she was usually the one to spearhead donations. A role she was much more comfortable with.

"There's also a room for you at The Alps should you and Megan need a place to stay," said Rose.

Carly felt her knees go weak. In the chaos, she'd forgotten all about Megan. What kind of mother did that? How would her daughter react? Would she be scared? Sad?

Andrew moved behind her then. Placed his warm, strong hands on her shoulders. "Thank you, Rose, but that won't be necessary. Carly and Megan can stay in my grandmother's house if need be."

Hillary's gaze zeroed in on Andrew. "Do I know you?"

Andrew shook his head. "I don't believe so." He extended his hand. "Andrew Stephens."

The woman Carly suspected to be somewhere around sixty cautiously accepted the offer. "Hillary Ward-Thompson." She let go, still scrutinizing Andrew. "You wouldn't be related to Clint Stephens, by any chance?"

"Yes, ma'am. He's my father."

Hillary's espresso eyes widened for a split second. "You favor him a great deal."

"So I've been told." Seemingly distracted, Andrew shot a glance toward the house before peering down at Carly. "It looks like the chief might be ready to talk with you."

"We won't keep you, dear." Rose's smile was a sad one as she moved forward for another hug. "I'll touch base with you later. Until then—" she let go "—you're in my prayers." Turning to leave, she patted Andrew on the arm. "I'm glad you're here."

"Thanks, Rose. So am I."

Carly was glad, too. Without him, she'd be curled up in a corner somewhere, bawling like a baby, clueless about what to do or where to turn. But why was *he* glad?

As the two women continued down the sidewalk, Ouray's fire chief, Mike Christianson, approached. "Good to see you again, Andrew." The two men briefly shook hands.

"You, too, Mike. I just wish it were under better circumstances."

Carly swallowed hard as her former schoolmate turned his attention to her. Now married with three kids, Mike was a good guy. She knew he wouldn't sugarcoat anything. Though the harsh reality was what she feared the most.

His features softened as his weary green eyes met hers. "The good news is that the fire never made it to the second floor."

Her shoulders relaxed. That meant her guest rooms were okay. But what about her and Megan's rooms on the first floor? The kitchen, parlor and family room?

"Most of the damage was confined to the kitchen and family room."

"How bad?" She absently rubbed her arms.

He hesitated, his gaze momentarily falling to the

ground before bouncing back to hers. "I'm afraid you're not going to be able to stay here for a while, let alone host any guests. Kitchen is a complete loss."

So far, Carly had managed to keep her nausea in check. Right about now, though, she was quickly losing that battle. She didn't know which was worse—not being able to stay at Granger House or not hosting any guests. No guests meant no income, but to have her home taken from her...

Where was that oxygen mask?

As though sensing she needed help, Andrew slipped his arm around her while he addressed Mike. "Do you know what caused the fire?"

Mike nodded, his lips pressed into a thin line. "As most often happens, it was a cooking fire."

Confused, Carly shook her head. "Cooking? But I wasn't— Oh, no." She felt her eyes widen. Stumbled backward, but Andrew held her tight. Her hand flew to her mouth, horror flooding her veins. "The chicken." The earth swirled beneath her. Sweat gathered on her upper lip. "I forgot." She looked at Mike without really seeing him. "And I went to the bank."

A churning vortex of emotions whirled inside her. A feeling she'd experienced only one other time in her life. The night she learned that Dennis had died. And just like that time, this was all her fault, and poor Megan would be the one paying the price for Carly's mistake.

Andrew recognized the self-reproach that settled over Carly the moment she learned the cause of the fire. He was all too familiar with the hefty weight of guilt. He'd carried it for the last two years, since the day he'd given work a higher priority than his dying mother. When he'd finally made it to her bedside, it was too late. He never got to say goodbye or tell her how much he loved her.

He shook off the shame as the fire trucks pulled away. He had to do everything he could to help Carly. He could never turn his back on her. Especially now.

Still standing in his grandmother's front yard, he eyed his watch. School would be letting out soon. And if Megan came walking up here, unaware of what had happened, Carly would blame herself even more.

He wasn't about to let that happen. "What do you say we go meet Megan?"

Carly's deep breath sent a shudder through her. "I guess that would be best. Give me an opportunity to prepare her before she sees the house."

As they walked in the direction of the school, the extent of Carly's nervousness became clearer. The constant *zip, zip, zip* sound as she fiddled with the zipper on her jacket was enough to drive anyone crazy.

Still a block away from the school, he touched a hand to her elbow to stop her. "Anything you care to discuss?"

Her blue eyes were swimming with unshed tears as she peered up at him, her bottom lip quivering. "What am I going to say to her? I mean, what if she hates me?"

Seeing her pain made him long to pull her into his arms. "Hates you? Why would Megan hate you?"

"Because the fire was my fault." She crossed her arms over her chest and held on tightly. "Because of me, my daughter won't be able to sleep in her own bed tonight. Won't be able—"

"Now hold on a minute." Using their height difference to his advantage, he glared down at her. "It's not like you meant to start that fire. Being absentminded one time does not make you a bad mom." Softening his tone, he reached for her good hand. "Instead of focusing on the bad, play up the good. She's nine years old. Kids that age love sleepovers, don't they? Tell her she gets to have an extended sleepover at my grandmother's."

Lifting only her eyes, she sent him a skeptical look. "That's the only good thing you could come up with?"

It did sound kind of lame. "Well, I haven't seen the extent of the damage yet, but it sounds like you might be getting a new kitchen, too."

"Like Megan's going to be impressed with that." She started walking again, shoving her hands into her pockets. "I'm just going to have to trust God to give me the words."

When they met Megan at the school, she was her typical exuberant self. Obviously no one had mentioned anything to her about the fire. In a town as small as Ouray, that was unusual. Good, but unusual nonetheless.

The kid walked between them, her purple backpack bouncing with each step. "Did you make cookies today?"

He glanced at Carly to find her looking at him, her expression teetering somewhere between nervous and petrified. Did she really believe her daughter would hate her?

Hoping to reassure her, he offered a slight smile and nodded, as if to say, *You can do this*.

She nodded back. "No, sweetie. There was a little problem at home today." Stopping, she looked into her daughter's eyes. "A big problem, actually. There was a fire. In the kitchen."

Confusion marred Megan's freckled face.

"The fire chief said we're going to have to stay somewhere else for a while."

Megan looked up at her mother through sad eyes. "Where?"

"At Livie's."

The girl turned to Andrew then. "But where will you stay?"

"At the ranch."

Her eyes went wide. "You have a ranch?"

"No. It's my dad's."

"Oh." Her gaze drifted away, then quickly shot back to him. "Can I see it sometime?"

He couldn't help laughing. Whoever said kids were resilient was right. "Sure."

Several minutes later, with gray clouds moving in from the west, hinting at snow, the three of them stood at the back of his grandmother's drive, staring at Granger House. The charred back door stood slightly ajar, windows in both the kitchen and family room were gone, and soot marked the window frames where the flames and smoke had attempted to reach the second floor.

Carly rested her hands upon Megan's small shoulders. The girl's blue eyes were wide, swimming with a mixture of disbelief and fear, her bottom lip showing the slightest hint of a tremor.

Poor kid. The fire hadn't just robbed her of her home. It had robbed her of her security, as well. He had to find a way to make her feel safe again. To protect both her and her mother from any more pain. And standing here staring at the ruins of their beloved home wasn't going to do that.

He rubbed his hands together. "It's getting chilly out." He stepped between the two females and Granger House. "I'll tell you what. Why don't you two go on inside my grandmother's house and make yourselves at home while I survey things at your place?"

Both sent him an incredulous look.

"The fire chief said it was fine. I'll just see what kind of damage we're talking about."

"I want to go with you." Carly looked at him very matter-of-factly. "I'm going to have to see it eventually. Might as well get it over with so I know what I'm up against."

"Okay." He still didn't think it was a good idea, but… "What about Megan?"

"I want to go, too."

Carly smoothed a hand over her daughter's strawberry blond hair. "Are you sure, sweetie?"

The girl nodded, not looking at all sure of anything.

"All right, then." Still skeptical, he went to his truck to retrieve some flashlights from the toolbox in the bed. With the electricity out, it was likely to be pretty dark in there. "We'll go through the front door. Perhaps you'll each want to gather up a few things."

"Such as?" Carly watched him as he pulled out the flashlights.

"Whatever you can think of. Clothes. Toiletries." Assuming they hadn't been consumed in the fire. "Things you use day to day." He closed the lid on the large metal box. "Okay, let's go before it gets dark."

The trio climbed the wooden steps onto the front porch.

As soon as Andrew pushed the antique door open, they were met with the strong odor of smoke.

"Eww…" Megan held her nose. "It stinks."

Carly put an arm around her. "I know, sweetie."

Inside, the parlor looked unscathed for the most part, save for the slight tinge of soot on the walls. He turned on his flashlight and aimed the beam around the room for a better look.

"Don't worry." He glanced at Megan now. "They have people who can take care of that and make everything smell like new."

"Really?"

Killing the light, he gave her his full attention. "Have I ever steered you wrong?"

That earned him a smile.

They moved collectively into the dining room, where

all the antique furniture appeared to be intact. But as they neared the door to the kitchen—

"Can I check my bedroom?" Megan's room sat off one end of the dining room, while Carly's was on the opposite end.

Carly glanced his way. "Would you mind going with her while I grab some things from my room?"

The fact that she trusted him with her daughter meant a lot. "Not at all."

Megan turned on her own flashlight and slowly moved into her room.

Andrew followed, relieved to see that, like the parlor and dining room, the mostly purple bedroom remained intact, though perhaps a little damp from all the water the firemen had used.

"Go ahead and take some clothes. I know they're probably wet or smell like smoke, but we can toss them in the wash."

While she opened drawers and pulled out items, all of which seemed to be purple or pink, with one random blue piece, he tugged the case from her pillow to hold the clothes.

"Oh, no."

He stopped what he was doing. "What is it?"

Head hung low, the girl frowned. "My cards. I left them in the family room."

If cards were her greatest loss, he'd count himself blessed. Still, they were important to her. "No worries. I'll pick you up a new deck tomorrow."

Her gaze shot to his. "Really?"

"Cross my heart—" he fingered an X across his chest "—and hope to die."

She threw her arms around his waist. "You're the best, Andrew."

The gesture stunned him. Or maybe it was the intense emotions her hug evoked in him. He'd never had much interaction with kids. But this one was definitely special.

A few minutes later, when he and Megan returned to the dining room with a pillowcase full of clothes and shoes, he dared what he hoped was a stealthy peek into the kitchen. And while it was too dark to see everything, what little he did glimpse didn't look good. Or even salvageable.

"Ah, good. You got some clothes." He jumped at the sound of Carly's voice. Turning, he saw her standing beside the table, holding a large tote bag.

"We did, so it looks like we're ready to go." He did not want to allow Carly in the kitchen. At least, not now. Maybe tomorrow, after the shock had a chance to wear off.

"Not yet." Carly set her bag atop the dining room table. "I'd like to see the kitchen."

"Let's do that tomorrow. It's getting dark outside anyway, so you won't be able to see much."

Leaving her bag behind, she took several determined steps toward him and stopped. "I want to see it. Now."

Chapter Five

Talking tough was one thing. Putting words into action was another. And try as she might, Carly couldn't persuade her feet to move across the wooden floorboards of her dining room. Still, she had to do this, had to see her kitchen, because not knowing left far too much to the imagination.

She drew in a bolstering breath, the sickening smell of smoke turning her stomach. At least her great-grandmother's dining room set and sideboard had been spared, as had the antique pieces in the parlor and her bedroom. Her gaze traveled to the opening that separated the dining room from the kitchen. Based on the charred swinging door, she doubted things on the other side of the wall had fared so well.

"You're sure you want to do this?" The uncertainty in Andrew's voice only solidified her determination.

"Yes." She eyed her daughter. "Megan, you stay with Andrew."

Willing one foot in front of the other, she eased toward the kitchen door, her mouth dry. Her heart thudded against her chest as though it were looking for escape.

The closer she drew to the kitchen, the more bleak things became. She reached out a steadying hand, only to have her fingers brush across the scorched casing that surrounded the door. Trim that was original to the house, now burned and blackened. And she had yet to see the worst of it.

Two more steps and she rounded into the kitchen. She clicked on the flashlight Andrew had given her.

Her heart, which had been beating wildly only seconds ago, skidded to a stop. The space was almost unrecognizable. Soot-covered paint peeled away from the walls, dangling in pathetic strips. Floors and countertops were littered with water-soaked ash and all kinds of matter she couldn't begin to identify or explain. She always kept a clean kitchen, so how could—?

Looking up, she realized the ceiling was gone. Over a hundred years of drywall, plaster and who knew what else now strewn across the room, exposing the still-intact floor joists of the bedroom above.

How could she have been so careless? This would take forever to fix. Where would she even begin?

The once dark stained cabinets that Carly had painted white shortly after taking over the house were blistered and burned. The butcher-block island top, salvaged from the original kitchen, had met a similar fate.

Noting her commercial range at the far end of the room, she tiptoed across the wet floor, tears welling as she ran her hand over the soot-covered stainless steel. It had been only two months since she'd paid it off.

"Mommy?"

She blinked hard and fast. She couldn't let Megan see her like this.

Turning, she saw her daughter standing in the doorway, lip quivering, holding up a blackened, half-melted blob of blue-and-white fur.

A sob caught in Carly's throat. Boo Bunny, Megan's

favorite stuffed animal. The one her father had given her, the one she still slept with every night.

As the cry threatened to escape, Carly pressed a hand to her mouth and quickly turned away. She'd failed her daughter not once but twice, throwing her life into a tail-spin from which she might never recover.

"Megan," said Andrew, "why don't we go outside and get some fresh air?"

Out of the corner of her eye, Carly saw Andrew escort her daughter from the room. She appreciated his interven-tion, as well as everything else he'd done for her today. Without his steadfast presence and guidance, she would be an even bigger mess.

After pulling herself together and taking a quick pe-rusal of the partially burned-out family room, she joined Andrew and Megan on the front porch. The two were sitting in the swing, and Carly was pretty sure she over-heard something about another game of cards. If it made her baby happy, she was all for it.

"Ready?" Andrew stood and handed Carly her tote.

"Yes."

"I'm hungry." Megan hopped out of the swing.

Peering at the sky, Carly was surprised to see that the sun had already dipped below the town's western slope. Though it wasn't dark yet, Ouray lay bathed in shadows. And her daughter had yet to have her after-school snack. Carly shook her head, disgusted. Add that to her list of failures.

A black, late-model SUV pulled alongside the curb just then, coming to a stop behind Carly's vehicle.

"Cassidy!" Megan bounded down the stairs as Celeste Purcell and her two daughters, Cassidy and Emma, got out.

Carly glanced back at Andrew, then tugged her tote over her shoulder and followed.

The three girls hugged and were practically giddy by the time she reached Celeste.

Her very pregnant friend met her with a sad smile. "Oh, Carly." They hugged best they could with Celeste's swollen belly between them. Then, with a final squeeze, Celeste stepped back, her brown eyes focused on Carly. "How bad is it?"

"Pretty bad." She drew in a shaky breath, still clueless about how to move forward. "At least the major damage was confined to the kitchen and family room."

Celeste pointed to Carly's tote bag. "Mom and Rose said you're going to stay next door."

"Yes, at Livie's house." She poked a thumb toward the home. "Andrew said— Oh, wait." She twisted to find Andrew standing behind her. "Celeste, this is Andrew Stephens. Andrew, Celeste Purcell."

"You were in the diner today." Celeste smiled.

He rocked back on his heels, Megan's pillowcase full of clothes at his feet. "I was. Good food, by the way."

"Speaking of food…" Celeste started toward the back of her vehicle, moving past the chattering trio of girls, to open the hatch.

The girls' giggles warmed Carly's heart. Perhaps her daughter would be okay after all.

Celeste tugged at a large box. "I brought you some enchiladas, chips and salsa for dinner and a pan of Granny's cinnamon rolls for breakfast." She started to lift the box, but Andrew intercepted her.

"Let me get that." He took hold of the cardboard container. "Smells fantastic."

Carly reached to close the hatch. "You didn't have to do all that, Celeste."

"Sweetie, if the roles were reversed, I know you'd be doing the same thing for me."

The crunch of gravel under tires drew their attention to the street.

The approaching Jeep eased to a stop in front of Livie's house. Blakely Lockridge, Rose's granddaughter, and Taryn Coble, Celeste's sister-in-law, soon emerged.

"Sorry we're late." Taryn tossed the driver's door closed behind her before falling in alongside Blakely. "I had to feed the baby."

"How is the little guy?" Carly eyed the new mother.

Taryn blushed. "He's just perfect."

"You won't be saying that once he starts walking." Blakely had a toddler herself, as well as an almost-teen. And Carly was pretty sure she'd heard recent mention of another one on the way. Her strawberry blonde friend addressed her now. "How are you holding up?"

"I'm still standing." Though given the opportunity, she was certain she could collapse at any moment.

"And we thank God for that," said Blakely.

"Mommy—" Megan tugged on Carly's jacket "—I'm hungry. Can the girls and I have a treat?"

Carly looked down at her daughter, her heart twisting. Other than what Celeste had brought, she had no food. Nothing to give her daughter, no—

"Oh, I almost forgot. There are some cookies in the box, too," said Celeste. "Help yourselves."

As Andrew pulled a plastic container from the box and handed it to Megan, Taryn said, "Blakes, that sounds like our cue to unload."

"Unload?" Carly watched the two women as they returned to Taryn's Jeep.

"We thought you might be in need of a few groceries." To emphasize her point, Blakely lifted two brown paper bags from the backseat.

Andrew nudged Carly with his elbow and nodded toward Livie's. "Would you mind catching the door?"

Celeste and her girls said goodbye as the rest of them made their way inside. In no time, every horizontal surface in Livie's kitchen, countertop and tabletop, was covered with bags and boxes. And the aroma of those enchiladas wafting from the oven had Carly's stomach growling.

Blakely emptied butter, eggs, fruits and vegetables from one bag and put them in the fridge. "We'll let everyone know where to find you, because there will be plenty more food."

"Oh, and Dad said to tell you he'll be by first thing tomorrow morning." Taryn folded an empty bag. Her father was Carly's insurance agent. "He was stuck in Grand Junction today. Otherwise he'd be here now. However, he's already contacted a restoration company out of Montrose, and they should be here anytime."

The outpouring of support had Carly feeling overwhelmed. She was blessed to have such wonderful friends. Yet as they continued to work, small arms worked their way around her waist, and she gazed down into her daughter's troubled blue eyes. Carly couldn't help worrying. While Megan had been able to laugh with the girls, reality had again taken center stage. Now it was up to Carly to make things better. And she'd do whatever it took to make that happen.

Andrew had forgotten how generous the people of Ouray could be. When cancer claimed his mother two years ago, the donations of food were almost more than his brothers and dad could eat. A scenario that had played out again when his grandmother died last fall.

He eyed the goodie-covered counter in his grandmother's kitchen, recalling that summer his dad had gotten pneumonia. Andrew was only fifteen at the time, his brother Noah, eighteen. That was the worst summer ever as the two of them worked the ranch without their father. Thanks to the town's generosity, though, their family never went hungry.

Now, seeing Carly the beneficiary of their goodwill warmed his jaded heart. He couldn't think of anyone more deserving. The outpouring of support also reminded him of how different Ouray was from the big city. Everyone banding together for the common good.

While Carly put Megan to bed, Andrew called his father and brought him up to speed, telling him about the fire and letting him know that he'd be staying at the ranch. Then he went to work, trying to clean up the kitchen and put away as many things as he could. Whatever would help Carly.

People had been stopping by all evening, dropping off casseroles, baked goods and groceries. Some had even gone so far as to bring clothes and toiletries—those things people used every day but didn't give much thought to until they didn't have them.

Glancing around the outdated room, he could hear the sound of a generator coming from next door. Per the insurance company, the restoration team had arrived from Montrose shortly after Blakely and Taryn had left. So when more people arrived with food, he took the opportunity to slip over to Granger House. The crew had immediately gone to work assessing the extent of the damage, not only from the fire but from smoke, soot and water, as well. They'd also begun the water removal process to prevent further damage and boarded up the back door and broken windows. This was only the beginning, though. Getting rid of all traces of smoke and soot would likely take weeks.

He shoved two more boxes of cereal into the already overstuffed pantry. Had it really been only yesterday that he left Denver? Closing the door, he shook his head. So much had transpired since then. Just thinking what lay ahead for Carly had his brain spinning. Though he doubted she had a clue.

Instead, her sole focus was her daughter, and rightfully so. But come tomorrow, she was going to be bombarded with a lot of things that would need to be addressed right away. And with Carly teetering on the brink of collapse, he couldn't help feeling that he should step in and help guide her through the aftermath. After all, he was a contractor, and she was…the woman he'd once planned to marry.

He closed the pantry door and leaned against it. They'd dated the last two years of high school and had their future planned out. Or so he'd thought. He went off to college in Denver, and she followed the next year. Then he left school in favor of the construction job he'd taken over the summer. The money was good, meaning they could marry sooner and start on a solid foundation, instead of struggling the way his parents had.

But between his work schedule and her classes, they rarely saw each other. Before he knew it, she was ready to go back to Ouray. Hoping she'd stay, he proposed. But she wasn't interested in building a life in Denver. And he had no interest in coming back to Ouray. His dreams were far too big for this small town.

Movement had him turning to see Carly coming into the kitchen. She looked like the walking dead. Only much prettier, of course.

She stopped abruptly, her weary gaze skimming the kitchen. "Where did everything go?"

"Pantry, cupboard—" he pointed "—pretty much any-place it would fit." He paused, suddenly second-guessing the decision. Who was he to organize someone else's kitchen? A woman's, no less. He was just a single guy whose refrigerator had more empty space than actual food. Besides, Carly probably had her own way of organizing. "You're welcome to move things wherever you like, though."

"No. I'm sure they're just fine where they are." Her tired blue eyes found his. "Thank you for doing that for me." Her praise did strange things to his psyche.

"Megan go to sleep okay?"

"Surprisingly. I was afraid we might have a problem without Boo Bunny, but she barely lamented not having it. At least, not once I told her I'd let her pick out a new stuffed animal at the toy store."

"I take it Boo Bunny was the blue-and-white blob she found at the house."

"Yes. Her father gave it to her."

"No wonder she was so attached." After a silent moment, he said, "They're still hard at work next door, so don't be surprised if you hear noises."

"How can they do that? I mean, there's no electricity."

Smiling, he eased toward her, wanting to prepare her for tomorrow. "That's what generators are for."

"Oh, yeah." She covered a yawn with her gauzed hand. "I forgot about that."

She was beyond exhausted.

Whatever he'd planned to talk to her about could wait until morning. Right now she needed sleep.

Moving into the living room, he picked up his duffel. "I should go so you can get some rest."

She didn't argue but followed him outside. "I figure one of two things will happen. Either I'll be asleep as soon as my head hits the pillow, or my mind will be so busy thinking about things that I won't get any sleep at all."

"Well, for your sake, I hope it's the first one." He looked up at the full moon high in the sky, illuminating the snow on the surrounding mountaintops.

The hum of the generator next door filtered through the cool air.

"What a difference twenty-four hours can make, huh?" There was a hint of hoarseness in Carly's voice.

Curious, he faced the woman who was now beside him.

"Last night at this time, I was slamming the door on you."

"Oh, that." He adjusted the duffel in his hand. "Well, this hasn't been what I would call an average day."

"No. Me, either." She rubbed her arms. "I appreciate everything you did for us today, Andrew."

"I didn't do much."

She peered up at him. "You were there for me. I needed that." With two steps toward him, she pushed up on her toes and hugged him around the neck. "Thank you." Her words were a whisper on his ear, soft and warm. And he felt his world shift.

Releasing him, she turned for the door. "Good night."

Still stunned, he managed to eke out "Night" before she disappeared into the house.

Climbing into his truck a few minutes later, he shoved the key in the ignition and waited for his breathing to even out. Carly stirred something inside him that he hadn't felt...well, since they were a couple.

That was not good. Because despite today's events, there was still the issue of his grandmother's house. And that was a battle he intended to win. Even with this little hiccup.

Shifting his truck into gear, he headed in the direction of the ranch. He had only eight weeks before he was needed back in Denver. After that, he didn't know when he'd be able to break away to work on Grandma's house. Which meant he had to settle the question of ownership quickly. Something Carly wasn't likely to discuss until

Granger House was up and running again. Meaning he'd have to see to it that the repairs didn't take any longer than necessary. And that left him with only one option.

He'd have to do the work himself.

Chapter Six

The air was crisp the next morning as Carly walked a seemingly rejuvenated Megan to school. After much reassurance that Granger House would not forever smell like smoke, her daughter was quick to offer up suggestions for both the kitchen and the family room. Starting with turquoise cabinets and a purple sofa.

Now, sitting at Livie's kitchen table, Carly couldn't help but chuckle. While those were indeed beautiful colors, they weren't exactly appropriate for a historic home such as Granger House.

Nursing her fourth cup of tea, she stared out the window at the large blue spruce that swallowed up much of the backyard. She'd spent half the night second-guessing her refusal of Andrew's offer to pay her full price for her half of this house. That would pay for Megan's college and then some.

But it would also mean giving up her dream. Something her brain was too muddled to think about right now. At this point, her mind couldn't fully process anything.

Regardless, her daughter's attitude this morning had apparently rubbed off on her. She was ready to roll up her sleeves and get busy on the repairs. Because the sooner that happened, the sooner she'd be back in business.

Her phone vibrated, sending it dancing across the table's wood veneer.

Picking it up, she saw her mother's number on the screen. She'd called her parents last night, after Andrew left, to tell them about the fire. So why was Mom calling now? Carly hoped she hadn't added to her mother's worry. After all, with Carly's father recovering from back surgery, the woman had enough on her plate.

"Hi, Mom." She pressed the device against her ear and took another sip of the English breakfast tea Blakely had so graciously brought her.

"Morning. I just wanted to check in and see how you were doing. Please tell me you were able to get some sleep. You sounded absolutely exhausted last night."

"I was." Too many crazy thoughts running through her head for any real sleep, though.

"You're still at Livie's, I take it."

"At the moment. I'm waiting for Phil so we can go over the insurance stuff."

"Oh, I so wish I could be there to help walk you through this mess."

"I'll be fine, Mom. Dad's health is far more important than holding my hand. Besides, I've got Phil and Andrew to help me."

"Be sure to tell Andrew we said thanks for letting you and Megan stay at Livie's."

"What do you mean thank him? I am part owner, you know."

"Okay, then tell him I appreciate all the support he's given you. Not every man would be willing to do that. Especially one you have a history with."

"Point taken." She still didn't know what she would

have done without him and was grateful she didn't have to find out. "Just so you'll know, I did thank him for his help."

"That's my girl."

The doorbell rang.

"I need to let you go, Mom." She stood and started toward the front door.

"Call me later?"

"I will."

"Love you."

She paused at the front door. "Love you, too." Ending the call, she shoved the phone in the back pocket of her jeans and tugged open the solid oak door. "Hi, Phil."

"Good morning." He wiped his feet on the mat before stepping inside. "Sounds like the restoration guys are hard at work next door."

She nodded, pushing the door closed. "I'm pretty sure they were here all night. Either that or they left late and were back at it by the time I took Megan to school."

"That's good. The sooner we jump on this, the better off you'll be."

"Amen to that." She pushed up the sleeves of her sweater, grateful her folks took care of the asbestos back in the eighties. Otherwise she'd have to wait weeks on abatement alone. "I am ready to put this behind me ASAP."

"In that case, shall we head next door?"

"Oh. Okay."

"You sound disappointed."

"No. I guess I just thought we'd have to go over my policy or something."

Feet shoulder width apart, the silver-haired man thumped his tablet against his thigh. "I've already done that. The damage and contents are covered, minus your deductible, of course."

"How much will that be?"

"Two percent of whatever the total is. I won't know for sure until I've assessed the damage."

Nodding, she mentally crunched some numbers. Looked like she'd have to tap into the money she'd planned to use to purchase the other half of Livie's house. Money that had originally been set aside for a kitchen reno. Talk about irony.

"You also have business interruption. That covers whatever profits would have been earned during the restoration process."

"Yes, I remember Dad insisting I put that in there."

Phil lifted a brow. "Aren't you glad he did?"

"Definitely." She again reached for the door. "I guess we'd best head on over to my house, then."

Outside, the restoration company's generator echoed throughout the neighborhood. The sun had risen higher in the sky, chasing away the early morning chill. As she approached Granger House, though, a dark cloud settled over her. Things had looked pretty bleak when she surveyed the damage last night. Now, in the light of day, they'd likely appear worse. She wasn't sure she could go through that again.

Do you want Granger House up and running or not?

She didn't have to think twice.

Drawing from the steely reserve that had served her in the past, she pushed through the front door. After a brief discussion with the restoration crew, she and Phil stood in her burned-out kitchen. With no heat and blowers going since last night to dry things out, the place was freezing. For now, at least, the blowers had been turned off.

A high-powered floodlight connected to a generator illuminated things as Phil moved about the room, taking measurements and making notes on his tablet. "I don't suppose you have an inventory of your belongings, do you?"

"Only the antiques." She rubbed her arms. "Why? Is that bad?"

"No." He sent her a reassuring smile. "It just means you'll have a little homework to do."

"Such as…?"

"You'll need to walk through each of these spaces mentally and write down everything that was in them. Everything from appliances to salt shakers. Storage containers, pots, pans, utensils…anything that was lost."

"I can do that."

"By the way, did you have any reservations on the books?"

Reservations? "How could I have forgotten something so important? I have bookings for this coming weekend and just about every weekend after that."

"I'm afraid you'll need to contact those people."

She blew out a frustrated breath. "I've got their information on my—" She gasped. Her laptop?

She hurried to the heavily charred table that now rested on two legs. "Where did it—?" Lowering her gaze, she spotted the half-open computer lying on the floor. Her heart sank as she lifted the partially melted, soot-covered device. The business she'd worked so hard to build was crumbling before her very eyes.

Feeling a hand on her shoulder, she looked into Phil's warm gaze.

"Do you have remote backup?"

Obviously she hadn't had enough tea. Or sleep. "Yes." Dennis had been a computer guru, so the concept of remote backup had been engrained in her.

Thank You, God.

"Good. We'll cover a new laptop." He took hold of the one she still held in her hand and set it aside. "In the meantime, I have one you can borrow. I'll bring it by later today." Turning, he continued. "The restoration company will clean everything in the house, from carpets to draperies to anything else that was affected by the smoke or water."

"That's good to know."

"Did you have a contractor in mind?"

"For what?"

"To do the work on your kitchen. Looks like you'll be getting a new one."

"Oh." While she supposed that was good news, she never realized there would be so many things to consider. "No. I—"

"Hello?" Andrew stepped into the kitchen. "I thought I might find you here." He continued toward them. "Phil. How's it going?" The two men shook hands.

"Good. How 'bout yourself?"

"Not too shabby." Wearing a lined denim jacket over a beige Henley, he rested his hands on his hips. "You two been going over everything?"

"Actually, I was just asking Carly about contractors."

"I guess I showed up at the right time, then." He smiled at Carly. "Since you and Megan will be staying at my grandmother's, that leaves me with nothing to do. So—" he shrugged "—I'd be happy to offer my services."

"Uh…" Working with Andrew? That would mean seeing him every day.

"I'd be able to start right away."

Phil's gaze darted between Carly and Andrew before settling on Carly. "A good contractor who can start immediately? That's pretty rare."

Probably. But still…

She crossed her arms over her chest. "What do you think it'll take? Two, three weeks?"

"More like five or six," said Andrew.

"Weeks?" Granger House couldn't be closed for that long. And she definitely wasn't willing to spend that much time with Andrew. She glanced at Phil, hoping he'd concur that five weeks was far too long.

"Sounds about right to me."

She felt her body sag. If that were the case, waiting for another contractor would only mean the project would take even longer. And she didn't want Granger House out of commission any longer than necessary.

But working with Andrew?

Seemed as though she didn't have a choice.

Squaring her shoulders, she looked him in the eye. "Have at it, then. The sooner things get started, the better off we'll both be." Because seeing Andrew, day in and day out, was the last thing she wanted to do.

Sunday afternoon, Andrew stood in the shell of Carly's kitchen, the space illuminated by portable floodlights he'd hooked up to a generator, awaiting her thoughts on her new kitchen layout. With the help of his younger brothers, Matt and Jude, along with Carly and even Megan, they'd gutted the space, removing everything from cupboards to appliances, debris, you name it. They salvaged what they could and tossed the rest into the Dumpster he'd had brought in.

On Friday, he went to the city to see about permits. To his surprise, they said he'd be able to pick them up Monday afternoon. Something that never would have happened in Denver. He grabbed his travel mug from atop his toolbox and took a swig of coffee. He was proud of Carly, the way she'd pulled herself up by her bootstraps and dug in to get the job done. Not everyone would have been able to bounce back so quickly. Then again, most people didn't have a kid like Megan to spur them on. She'd definitely kept things lively during the demo, chattering almost nonstop about school, her friends and how the fire had practically made her a celebrity.

Shaking his head, he chuckled. Megan was a great kid. In some ways much like her mother, while in others quite different. Like her outgoing personality. Growing up, Carly had definitely leaned more toward the timid side. Something she'd obviously grown out of.

He was glad he was able to help them. Even if his motives weren't as pure as they should have been. Working on Carly's place also gave him an excuse not to be at the ranch. It wasn't that he didn't love his father. On the contrary, he rather enjoyed spending time with him. The old man was always up for a good conversation. But the ranch was so…depressing. Sometimes he felt as though the place just sucked the life right out of him. Like it had his mother.

Shaking off the morbid thought, he turned off the noisy blowers the restoration company had kept going almost from the moment they arrived, then glanced at his watch before strolling into the dining room. Where was Carly?

He'd told her that, since they were starting from scratch, she was free to do just about anything she wanted in terms of layout. Instead of sharing her thoughts, though, she'd paced the wooden floor virtually the entire weekend, tapping a finger to her pretty lips as she hemmed and hawed.

Well, now he needed some decisions so he could get the ball rolling first thing tomorrow.

Just when he was about to head next door to check on her, she strolled through the front door, looking much cuter than most of his clients.

"Sorry I'm late." Her blond curls bounced around her shoulders. "Someone called wanting to make reservations for this summer."

With Granger House Inn's landline out, she'd been able to get calls forwarded to her mobile phone.

Hands tucked in the pockets of her fleece jacket, she shrugged. "It felt good to *book* a reservation instead of canceling." Reluctantly she'd contacted all of her upcoming clients, letting them know about the fire and offering them a discount on a future stay. Even though her insurance policy had coverage for business interruption, he knew she was worried about Granger House Inn's reputation and felt the incentive might help smooth things over.

"Well, then, I guess we'd better get going on things. Can't have a bed-and-breakfast without a kitchen." Besides, the faster he finished Carly's house, the faster he could move on to his grandmother's. Though he still might not complete it before heading back to Denver.

Of course, that was assuming he and Carly could come to an agreement. But that was a discussion for another day.

"Where's Megan?" he tossed over his shoulder on his way into the kitchen.

"At a friend's."

Once inside the space that had been stripped to the studs, some of which were damaged by the fire and would have to be replaced, he clapped his hands together and rubbed them vigorously. "Okay, so what are we doing?"

Carly opened her mouth as though she were ready to share her vision, then snapped it shut, her shoulders drooping. "I don't know."

He tamped down his rising frustration. "Carly, you spend a lot of time in this room and do a *lot* of cooking. Haven't you ever dreamed of having more counter space or better lighting? More storage?"

"Yes. At one time, I was even saving to have the kitchen remodeled. Then I got the news from the lawyer about your grandmother's house and my plans changed." She met his gaze. "Still, I never had any really cohesive plans."

"But it's a starting place." He took a step closer. "Tell

me what some of your thoughts were. Some of the things you were wanting."

"That's just it. My thoughts are too jumbled together right now for me even to begin to sort them out. It's like somebody just dumped a five-thousand-piece puzzle in front of me and told me to put the thing together without ever looking at the box cover. The only things I know for sure are that I want a kitchen that is efficient and looks like it belongs here. Nothing ultracontemporary or trendy." Suddenly a bit more animated, she started to pace. "I want classic. And white. Something nice and bright."

Efficient and classic. Now they were getting somewhere. "Hmm… Megan's going to be one disappointed little girl."

Carly turned to look at him.

"She's pretty stoked about the turquoise, you know?"

That earned him a laugh. And hopefully lightened her mood.

"Now let's talk layout," he continued. "Where would you like to put the sink?"

Her brow puckered in confusion. "Right where it's always been. I mean, you can't just move a sink."

He couldn't help smiling. "Yes, believe it not, you can. Especially in a situation like this, when you're starting from scratch. All we have to do is move the plumbing."

"You can do that?"

"With the help of a licensed plumber, yes." He crossed the room, his work boots thudding against the floorboards. "What would you think about putting it here, under the window?" He stood in front of the currently boarded-up opening. "That way, instead of looking at a blank wall while you're doing dishes, you can look outside."

Her nose scrunched. "That would be better. But then, what would I put where the sink used to be?"

Good grief. Had she never watched HGTV?

He moved back to where she stood. "Are you familiar with the kitchen work triangle?"

"Sort of, yes. Sink, stove, fridge, right?"

"Exactly. So rather than having your stove way over on the other side of the room—which was an obvious afterthought—what if we put it where the sink used to be?"

Her blue eyes scanned the room. "What would you think about using some vintage and reclaimed pieces? Cabinets, perhaps?"

He kept his groan to himself. The search for those items could take forever, leaving him no time to work on his own planned renovations. Watching Carly wander the kitchen, though, her thoughts finally taking flight, he couldn't help being drawn in. The sparkle in her eyes made it impossible. Instead, he found himself wanting to make her dreams come true. Even if she wasn't sure what those dreams were.

"What would you think about adding a pantry? And a bigger island? One people could sit at."

Her expression unreadable, she simply blinked. "That would be amazing. But how?"

"Carly, this is a *big* space." He stretched his arms wide. "Don't confine yourself to the way things used to be. You said you wanted to expand the B and B. Here's your starting point." Considering he still had no plans to budge on Grandma's house, he probably should have phrased that differently. But the faster she moved, the faster he could get back to working on his own project.

"We can do this, Carly. Together." He took a step closer. "So what do you say? Shall we take a chance on something new and fresh?"

Chapter Seven

Thanks to the wonderful people at the local internet provider, Carly no longer had to tote Phil's laptop to the local coffee shop for access. Instead, she could remain at Livie's and surf the web to her heart's content. And ever since her meeting with Andrew last night, she'd done just that. However, her heart was anything but content. On the contrary, the countless hours spent staring at the computer screen, looking at Victorian-era kitchens, trying to decide what she wanted, had only confused her more. Sure, she'd seen a lot of things that looked great, but how would they work for her?

Having Andrew breathing down her neck wasn't helping any, either. She knew she needed to make a decision, but a kitchen was a long-term commitment. One she had no intention of rushing into, regardless of how hard he pushed. A well-thought-out kitchen took a lot of careful planning. After all, it wasn't simply a room. It was an extension of her. And if past experience was any indication, it's where she'd be spending most of her time. So she was determined to get it right.

If only she were able to envision what the finished product would look like. The images she'd seen online gave her some clue, but she had yet to find a kitchen the size of hers. And that only added to her frustration.

In the meantime, Andrew was awaiting her decision. "Cabinets alone can take up to six weeks to come in," he'd said.

Did he think she was purposely dragging her feet? That she wasn't eager to get back into her house?

Pushing away from Livie's kitchen table, she went to the counter and poured herself another cup of tea. *God, I could really use a heaping helping of clarity here.*

A knock sounded at the door.

Cup in hand, she made her way to the front door and tugged it open to find a smiling Andrew. As if she needed any more pressure.

"What are you doing?" He followed her back into the kitchen.

Tucking her irritation aside, she pointed to the laptop. "Same thing I've been doing for two days."

"Any progress?"

She set her mug on the table and glared at him. "No. And I'd appreciate it if you would stop bugging me about it. When I make a decision—"

"Get your coat. We're going to get you some help."

Her gaze narrowed on him. "What? You're taking me to a shrink?"

"No. I'm taking you someplace where they will help you visualize your new kitchen."

He was taking her. Did he think she was incapable of making a decision on her own? Not that she didn't appreciate all of his hard work and persistence. Without his take-charge attitude, her kitchen would still be in shambles.

Still, she'd learned the hard way that the only one she could truly count on was herself. She was the one who had to live with her choice, not Andrew. Besides, all of this togetherness was getting a bit unnerving.

What are you afraid of? Andrew is nothing more than an old friend.

Yeah, a really cute old friend.

You wanted to know what your new kitchen was going to look like.

She huffed out a breath. "Okay, let's go."

Forty-five minutes later, he pulled his truck up to a kitchen design showroom in Montrose.

Inside, there were kitchen vignettes, all in different styles. Some were sleek and contemporary, while others were rustic. Still others leaned more toward the classic look.

"Welcome to Kitchen and Bath Showcase." A petite saleswoman Carly guessed to be not much older than her thirty-six years approached, her high-heeled pumps tap, tap, tapping against the gleaming tile floor. "I'm Marianne."

"Hi, Marianne." Andrew extended his hand. "Andrew Stephens. We spoke earlier this morning."

"Yes." Her gaze moved to Carly. "Andrew tells me you're having some problems visualizing your new kitchen."

"I'm a bit overwhelmed, yes."

"That's entirely understandable. And exactly why we're here." Marianne gestured toward the kitchen displays to their left. "Let's take a stroll over here." She led them into the maze of sample kitchens. "I understand you have a Victorian home."

"That's correct. So I don't want anything contemporary."

"Oh, no. A Victorian demands something timeless."

Timeless? That would work.

Marianne led them past a vignette with knotty wood cabinets, black countertops and a rustic wood floor. "Are you thinking stained or painted cabinetry?"

"Painted. I want light and airy."

"Something like this?" Marianne motioned to an all-white kitchen with a dark wood floor that warmed the whole space.

"Wow." Carly stepped onto the hardwood. Smoothed a hand across the beautiful island topped with Carrara marble. The cupboards were simple. Classic. And she liked the white subway tile backsplash.

"Marianne, did you receive the pictures and dimensions that I emailed you?" Andrew was beside Carly now.

"I did, and I already have them plugged into my computer. Once we settle on a few things, we can get to work."

"What do you think, Carly?"

She tried to ignore the feel of his hand against the small of her back and concentrated on the kitchen. "It's exactly what I want. But I still can't envision the layout."

"Come with me." Marianne motioned for them to follow.

On the opposite end of the showroom, Carly and Andrew settled in on one side of a long desk while Marianne pecked away at her computer on the other side until she'd pulled up a screen with the outline of Carly's kitchen. Everything from windows to doors was marked out.

"What I was thinking—" Andrew pointed at the large monitor "—was that we put the sink under the window on this wall, the stove over here—" he pointed again "—and then in this corner, a nice walk-in pantry."

"Were you wanting an island?" Marianne addressed Carly.

"Definitely. Granger House is also a bed-and-breakfast, so I need lots of counter space for prep work."

"I was thinking a large one about here." Andrew circled his finger in the open space across from the sink. "Perhaps with some seating."

"I have an idea." Marianne moved her mouse to direct the cursor on the computer screen. "Where does this door lead?"

"To the dining room," said Carly.

"If we put the sink on that wall under the window, your guests will be able to see the dirty dishes."

Carly leaned in closer. "You're right. I hadn't thought about that." Not exactly something she wanted her guests to see.

"So what if, instead of putting the sink here—" the woman made a few clicks on her mouse "—we leave that as a long counter you can use as a staging area?"

Carly straightened. "That would be amazing. But what about—?"

"The sink?" Marianne smiled. "You've definitely got enough room for an oversize island." She drew that out on the screen. "You could have seating on the far side. Over here, across from the stove, you could have your sink and dishwasher, and you'd still have plenty of countertop between the two for prepping food, rolling out dough, whatever."

Carly was getting more excited by the minute. But never had she been more thrilled than when Marianne typed everything into her computer and showed her an image of her new kitchen. No more guesswork or wondering. She could see everything for herself.

"That's amazing. I never would have thought I could have something like that. I won't know what to do with all that storage."

"Believe me, you'll figure it out." Marianne pushed

away from her desk. "Let's go look at some door samples and colors."

On the drive back to Ouray, Carly felt as though the weight of the world had been lifted off her shoulders. "I'm so glad you took me there, Andrew. Thank you."

"You're welcome." Hands on the steering wheel, he stared straight ahead.

Watching him, Carly realized he'd been the answer to her prayer. This trip had given her the clarity she'd asked God for this morning. She pressed against the leather seat of his truck, wondering again where she would be without him. He'd been her rock this past week, supporting her, guiding her through all the chaos. Something she never would have expected. Even from her husband.

Suddenly sullen, she turned away and looked out the window at the mountains that loomed in the distance. By their fifth wedding anniversary, Dennis had lost interest in their marriage. In her. Even with Megan in the picture, his work at a local internet technology firm took a higher priority than family. Customers demanded his time and got it. Leaving little to nothing for her and Megan.

Never again would she take second place in someone's life. If she ever fell in love again—which she had no intention of doing—she'd take first place or nothing at all.

Andrew awoke Tuesday morning, ready to get to work on Carly's kitchen. He was glad he'd taken her to the design showroom. He understood that some people had trouble visualizing things. And when talking about something as expensive as a kitchen, you wanted to get it right. But thanks to Marianne, Carly now knew exactly how her new kitchen was going to look.

He'd need to stop by the hardware store before he could get started, though. At first he thought that would require another trip to Montrose. Then his brother Noah reminded him there was now one in Ouray.

Armed with electrical wire and boxes, he exited the store, feeling more invigorated than he had in a long time. Probably because he'd spent far more time in the board-room than on the job site this past year.

The cool morning air swirled around him as he eyed the snow-covered peaks that enveloped the town and the rows of historic buildings up and down Main Street. For the most part, Ouray looked the same as it always had. Growing up, he'd felt as though Ouray held him back. There was a lot he wanted to achieve. But the tiny town had so little to offer that he couldn't wait to break free. Yet something about the town now felt…different. Less constricting.

Shrugging off the weird vibe, he loaded the supplies into his truck and headed for Granger House.

Aided by the floodlights, he spent the rest of his morn-ing swapping out the damaged studs and marking off the layout of the new kitchen. Since Marianne had flagged their cabinet order as expedited, he hoped they'd be able to shave some time off the six-week turnaround. Before cabinets, though, the kitchen's original hardwoods would need to be sanded, stained and sealed. Something that would prevent anyone from working in the kitchen for as much as a week while things dried.

However, there was plenty to do before then.

With the studs in place, he began drilling holes for the new wiring. He sure hoped Carly showed up soon. He was starving. But also grateful that she'd volunteered to feed him. Otherwise he'd have to make a run somewhere to grab something, and that would only take more time.

Since he'd turned off the blowers, he was able to hear when the front door opened.

"Get it while it's hot." Carly entered the kitchen carrying a brown paper bag in one hand and a thermos in the other.

He stopped what he was doing and set his drill on the floor. "You don't have to tell me twice."

"Good." Looking particularly pretty in a soft purple sweater that brought out her eyes, she set the items atop his makeshift worktable that consisted of two sawhorses and a sheet of plywood. "I've got grilled cheese on rye and some homemade tomato soup."

"Perfect." Especially since the house was still without heat.

She pulled two foil-wrapped sandwiches from the bag. "I didn't know how hungry you'd be, so I made you a second if you want it."

His stomach chose that moment to rumble.

Carly grinned, reaching for the old-fashioned thermos she must have found hidden away at his grandmother's. "It's in the bag whenever you're ready." She removed the lid, which functioned as a cup, and poured in the hot, steaming liquid. "Here you go."

"Thanks." His fingers brushed hers as he took hold of the cup. Their gazes collided, triggering the strangest sensation. Something akin to an electrical jolt. And judging by the way Carly quickly pulled away, her cheeks pink, he guessed she'd felt it, too.

He took a bite of his sandwich, chalking the whole thing up to static electricity.

Looking at everything in the room except him, she picked up her sandwich, peeled back the foil and took a dainty bite.

"I'll be starting on the electrical shortly," he said between bites. "If everything goes according to plan, drywall should be going up by the end of the week." He was rambling when he needed to shut up and eat.

"What about windows?" Setting her sandwich on the work table, she pointed to the boarded-over spaces where the windows and the back door once were.

"Thanks for the reminder. I was going to ask if you wanted to stick with the same size windows or, in the case of the one over here—" he moved to where he'd once suggested they put the sink "—would you like to go with something bigger?"

"Wouldn't bigger look out of place with the rest of the house?"

"Yes. So rather than go bigger with the actual window, we would simply add another window or even a third, like they did in other parts of the house."

"But what about the inside? The casings and such?"

"Not to worry. I spoke to Jude about it when we were doing the demo, and he said he could easily duplicate what's there now so everything would be seamless." When not on duty, his policeman brother was an extremely talented woodworker.

Carly didn't respond. Merely roamed the space, one arm crossed over her midsection, her other elbow resting on it as she tapped a finger to her lips. A stance that meant she was thinking about something. And usually spelled trouble for him. Was it the window she was thinking about or something more?

"I don't know about having the sink on the island. I mean, it's always been over here." She gestured to the wall behind her.

"Facing a blank wall." Sandwich in hand, he stepped closer. "Now you'll be able to see your entire kitchen when you're at the sink. Not to mention into the family room. You'll be able to see Megan."

"True. But I'm not sure how I feel about having the refrigerator at the far end of that counter. I'm used to having it closer to the dining room."

"It's not that much farther. And remember, you've got a bigger island now." Wadding up the foil from his first sandwich, he moved beside her. "It's a little late to start second-guessing things, Carly. The cabinets are already on order."

"Yes, but better to make changes now than later."

Why did she have to make any changes at all? "I thought you liked the new design." She was so excited when she saw the mock-up on the computer.

"I do. But it's so…different." She started pacing again. "What if I don't like it?"

"Look, I know you're afraid of change, but believe me, change can be good."

She whirled toward him then. And if looks could kill… "I am *not* afraid of change. But we're talking about a lot of money here, and I want to make sure I get things right."

"Whoa, easy." Holding his hands up, he took a step back. Why was she suddenly so defensive? "I'm not trying to cause any trouble."

His ringtone sounded from his jeans pocket.

He tugged out the phone and looked at the screen. His attorney. "Excuse me." He turned away. "Hey, Ned."

"I've got the latest numbers for Magnum Custom Home Builders."

Just what he'd been waiting for. "And?"

"Looks good. Matter of fact, real good."

"Gross profit?"

"Seven figures."

"Impressive." He glanced behind him to find Carly still wandering. "What kind of debt are we looking at?"

Ned rattled off the numbers.

"Not bad. Any property for future development?"

"Yes, though I don't have the details."

This time when he turned, he found Carly glaring at him. "Hey, I need to go, Ned. I'll touch base with you later." He ended the call and drank the last of his soup before approaching Carly. "Now, where were we?"

Arms crossed over her chest, nostrils flared, she said, "Everything is about money with you, isn't it?"

"What are you talking about? I'm purchasing a new business."

"Even back in high school, you were consumed with money."

"Yeah, so I could help my parents. You know better than anyone how they struggled to make ends meet."

"So you say."

He wasn't sure what had gotten under her skin, but she sure seemed eager to push his buttons.

He took a step closer until they were toe to toe. "Noah and I worked ourselves to death. Yet it wasn't enough. So forgive me if I refuse to struggle like my parents did." He turned away then, trying to ignore the pain and regret welling inside him.

"Funny, I never heard your parents complain. And why would they? I mean, five sons, a thriving ranch… Sounds to me like your folks had a pretty good life."

He jerked back around. "Then why did my mother die so young?"

Chapter Eight

Gray skies and freezing temperatures were the perfect match for Carly's mood. Standing outside Ouray's one and only school, she burrowed her hands deeper into the pockets of her coat, trying to get warm while she waited for Megan. More than three hours after she stormed out on Andrew, she still felt like a heel. She'd foolishly lashed out at him after he accused her of being afraid of change. He had no idea that those words would haunt her to her grave. That those same words were the reason she lost her husband.

She huffed out a breath and watched as it hung in the air. Somehow she had to make things right. Because the anguish on Andrew's face when he mentioned his mother still gnawed at her. She'd wanted to hurt him the way he'd hurt her. Apparently she'd succeeded. Now she was wrestling with herself, trying to come up with some way to make up for being so callous.

"It's f-f-freezing," said Megan several minutes later on their walk home.

"I told you it was going to get cold. But no…you refused to listen to your old mother and chose to wear your spring jacket."

Megan giggled. "Come on, Mom. You're not old."

Did the kid know how to get on her good side or what? "Well in that case—" she wrapped an arm around her daughter "—I've got some hot cocoa for you when we get home."

"What are you waiting for, then?" Megan took off running. "Come on."

When they reached Livie's house, Andrew was loading his truck. After a quick glance their way, he turned and stalked up the front steps and into Carly's house, shoulders slumped, looking every bit as miserable as he had when she left him.

She patted Megan on the shoulder. "You go on in. I'll be there shortly."

"What about the cocoa?"

"It's in the pan on the stove."

Megan's eyes widened. "Mom, you didn't—"

"No, I didn't leave the stove on. Pour some into a mug and then heat it in the microwave for a minute and a half."

"One, three, zero?"

"You got it."

Her daughter darted toward the house.

"There are some cookies on the counter, too."

A smiling Megan shot her a thumbs-up as she pushed through the door.

Carly tugged at the crocheted scarf around her neck and started next door as Andrew emerged from Granger House, carrying his toolbox. "How's it going?"

He shrugged. "Wiring's done."

"Sounds like progress." She shuffled her feet, waiting for him to respond, but he didn't. So much for small talk. *What do you expect after the way you went after him?* She moved to the far side of the truck where he stood, arms resting on the side of the pickup bed. "Look, I'm sorry for what I said earlier. I had no right to attack you like that."

He looked at her now, pain still evident in his dark eyes. "So, why did you?"

She swallowed hard. She couldn't tell him about Dennis. That she was the reason he was dead. Hands shoved in her pockets, she toed at the gravel in the drive. "Stress, I guess."

He nodded. "I can understand that."

He could?

"I know I can't take back what I said, but I'd like to make a peace offering in the form of dinner."

He lifted his head to stare at the darkening clouds. "I'm not really in the mood—"

"I brought you some hot cocoa, Andrew."

They turned to see Megan moving ever so slowly toward them, now wearing her winter coat, a steaming mug cradled in her mitten-covered hands.

He whisked past Carly to her daughter and took hold of the cup. "I was just thinking how nice it would be to have a hot cup of cocoa. How did you know?"

Megan's smile grew bigger by the second. "I don't know. I just did."

He took a sip. "Mmm…this is really good."

"My mommy makes the best cocoa. She says it's a secret recipe."

Carly felt herself blushing when he glanced at her.

"I was just asking Andrew if he'd like to join us for dinner." She knew she was playing dirty, basically suggesting her daughter help coerce him, but she couldn't help herself.

True to form, Megan bounced up and down, hands clasped together. "Oh, please say yes. I want to play cards again."

Carly had been grateful, if not a little surprised, when

Andrew presented Megan with a new deck the day after the fire. Megan had told her he said he would, yet Carly still doubted. The gesture had taught her that, among other things, Andrew was a man of his word.

He looked at Carly for a moment as though weighing his options. Or trying to come up with a way out. Finally he met Megan's gaze. "What time should I be here?"

Carly was glad he accepted her invitation. However, when he showed up at Livie's shortly after six, as opposed to the six thirty she'd suggested, she could have kicked herself for allowing Megan to go to a friend's. Because if she knew her daughter, she'd be home precisely at six thirty and not a minute before. Leaving Carly alone with Andrew until then.

"Make yourself at home," she tossed over her shoulder on her way back through Livie's parlor after answering the door. Her steps slowed as she approached the kitchen, though. This *was* his home. Half of it, anyway. Seemed her thoughts of a buyout and renovations had taken a backseat since the fire. Still, that didn't mean she was ready to give up on her dream.

Standing at the avocado-green stove, her back to him, she could feel him watching her. Normally being alone with him wouldn't have been a big deal. They'd actually been getting along quite well. But after putting her foot in it this afternoon…

"So, you're buying another business?" She turned.

He stood at the end of the peninsula, making an otherwise bland brown flannel shirt look incredible. "Yes. A custom home builder."

She retrieved three plates and three bowls from the cupboard, feeling like an even bigger jerk for tearing into him. "I imagine you're grateful to have some time off, then."

She breezed past him on her way to the table. "You know what they say about all work and no pla—"

One of the so-called unbreakable plates slipped from her hand then, crashing to the floor and shattering into a million tiny pieces.

Gasping, she slowly set the remaining dishes onto the table and stared at the shards splayed across the gold-and-brown vinyl floor, all around her socked feet.

"Don't move." Andrew was beside her in a flash. "Are you okay? You're not cut, are you?"

She shook her head, still shocked. That plate had virtually exploded. "I don't think so."

"Good." He studied the mess. "Let's try to keep it that way."

She sent him a curious glance. "What do you have in mind?"

"Only one thing I can think of." With that, he scooped her into his arms and started into the living room, the pieces of glass grinding beneath his work boots.

"Really? This is your only solution?" Resting one hand against his chest, she could feel his muscles. "You couldn't have simply swept up the stuff around me?"

His grin was a mischievous one. "Why would I do that when this is so much more fun?"

"Fun for you, maybe. For me, it's just—" *Torture* was the only word that came to mind. Being in Andrew's arms felt so…good.

"Just what?" In the parlor, he had yet to put her down. "I—I…"

His playful smile morphed into something different. More intense. His gaze probed hers, questioning. As if…

Her gaze drifted to his lips, though she quickly jerked them back to his eyes. The corners of his mouth tilted upward as if he knew what she was thinking.

The front door burst open. "It's snowing!"

They turned to see a stunned Megan.

Andrew quickly set Carly's feet on the hardwood floor.

Carly smoothed a hand over her sweater. Lost in Andrew's embrace, she'd forgotten all about the time.

A quick glance at Andrew revealed how red his face was. And if the heat in her own cheeks was any indication, she was just as crimson.

Megan's eyes narrowed for a second before she crossed her arms. "Were you guys kissing?"

"No," said Andrew.

"Of course not," Carly added.

Without further discussion, Andrew promptly returned to the kitchen and went to work sweeping up the broken glass, allowing Carly to get dinner on the table. And, fortunately, Megan let the subject drop. Likely because she was more interested in the card game Andrew had promised her after dinner.

"Come on, Mom. You need to play, too." Megan dutifully wiped off the freshly cleared table.

"But what about the dishes?" Carly turned on the water at the sink.

"Don't worry." Sitting in his chair, Andrew shuffled a deck of cards. "They'll still be there when we're done." His grin had her narrowing her gaze.

"Great." She turned off the water, and returned to her seat. "You'll be able to help me, then." Or maybe not. That would only keep him here longer, and they'd had enough togetherness today.

"Megan—" he watched Carly as she tossed the dishrag into the sink "—would you mind grabbing a couple of spoons?"

"What for?"

"I'm going to teach you a new game."

Her daughter's nose wrinkled. "With spoons?"

"I remember that game." Carly had played it many times with Andrew's family. "There are only three of us, though."

He leaned closer. "Figured we'd start her off slow."

Recalling the oft raucous times they used to have at the ranch, she said, "Good idea."

Andrew dealt the cards and explained the rules to her eager daughter. The first person to get four of a kind and grab a spoon was the winner.

Things were rather timid the first couple of rounds. Then it was a free-for-all until Megan and Andrew were fighting over the same spoon. Carly watched with amusement as her daughter stood beside him, wrestling the utensil from his hand.

"No…" He threw his head back. "It's mine, I tell ya. I was first."

Megan giggled, tugging with all her might. "Uh-uh."

Finally he relinquished the trophy, as Carly knew he would. What she hadn't counted on, though, was his laughter. Carefree and unrestrained, like when they were kids.

Making her laugh, too.

Gasping for air, he looked at her, his smile pensive. "Do you know how long it's been since I've done that?"

She wasn't sure if he was talking about the game or the laughter. Nonetheless, she said, "It's often the simple things that bring us the greatest pleasure."

"In that case, this is the greatest pleasure I've had in a long time."

She believed him. And that made her very sad.

Three days after Andrew had literally swept Carly off her feet, the aroma of her tropical shampoo still lingered in his mind.

And that was not a good thing. He was still thankful Megan had walked in when she did. Otherwise, he might have done something foolish, like kiss Carly. And that would have been a mistake. A relationship between them would never work. He was Denver, she was Ouray, and that's the way they would always be.

Yet as he pulled up to his grandmother's house Friday morning, he couldn't stop thinking about that game of Spoons and the pleasure it had brought him. It had been a long time since he'd done something just for fun. Work consumed most of his time. Then he'd go home to an empty house and collapse into bed. But now he found himself wondering—what if he had someone to go home to? A family. How different might his life look then?

Not that it mattered. He was a confirmed bachelor. One who needed to pull himself together, gather his thoughts and concentrate on today's mission. He was taking Carly and Megan, who was out of school for a teacher in-service day, on another trip to Montrose. This time they'd be looking at appliances, lighting, carpeting for the family room and such. Unlike yesterday, when they'd gone to choose the marble slabs for her countertops, nothing was needed immediately, but knowing how overwhelming the process could be, he thought it would be a good idea to get Carly started now.

A fresh dusting of snow covered the ground as he stepped out of his truck into the chilly midmorning air. Though with the sun coming out, it was likely to be gone by afternoon. Just as it had vanished earlier in the week.

It still surprised him that Megan wanted to go with them. Then again, after walking in on him and Carly the other night, she might have thought they needed a chaperone.

He continued up the walk and knocked on the door.

Megan opened it a few seconds later, already wearing her coat. "Hi."

"Hi, yourself. Looks like you're ready to go." Movement had his gaze shifting past her to her mother.

"We sure are." Wearing her puffy white jacket, Carly joined them.

"Okay, let's get on down the road, then."

They piled into his truck and pulled out of the drive.

He'd just turned onto Main Street when his phone rang through the truck's speakers and the name Dad appeared on the dashboard's touch screen caller ID.

He pressed the button on his steering wheel. "What's up, Dad?"

"You still in Ouray?" His father's deep voice boomed through the cab of the vehicle.

"Yes, sir."

"Carly and Megan with you?"

He glanced at Carly in the passenger seat and smiled. "Yes."

"Hi, Mr. Clint," yelled Megan from the backseat.

The familiarity surprised Andrew. Between Grandma and church, he supposed their families had always been intertwined.

"Morning, darlin'. Tell Andrew he needs to bring you and your mama by the ranch on your way to Montrose. I got somethin' I want to show you."

Andrew struggled to come up with what that something might be. His father was gone when he left that morning, and they hadn't spoken. But recalling how eager Megan was to visit the ranch…

"Okay, Dad. We're on our way."

"Abundant Blessings Ranch." Megan read the sign as they pulled onto the property. "This is where you grew up?"

Unfortunately. "I did."

She scooted to the driver's side of the truck and pressed her hands against the glass. "Cool. You have horses."

"Well, my brother and my dad do, anyway."

Megan's head poked between the two front seats. "Where's your mom?"

The question took him by surprise. Somehow he managed to keep it together, though. "She died."

"Oh, yeah." She lowered her head. "I forgot." When she looked up again, she said, "My daddy died."

He was taken aback by her candor. Not a hint of sorrow or regret. Then again, she was young when her father passed away. Not old enough to have regrets.

"Looks like the barn could use a fresh coat of paint." Leave it to Carly to take the subtle approach.

He glanced her way. "Or a demolition crew."

Dad emerged from the barn as Andrew pulled his truck up to the house.

Megan was the first to open her door and hop down onto the gravel. "Hi, Mr. Clint." She waved.

His father coughed as he approached. "Young lady, I think you've grown six inches since the last time I saw you." Which most likely would have been at church.

The kid grinned, straightening to her full height. All four-foot-whatever inches of her.

Carly stepped forward to hug the old man. "How are you, Clint?"

"Not too bad." Releasing her, he smiled, his dark gaze sparkling as it met each one of theirs. "Come with me. I've got something to show you."

Andrew couldn't help wondering what his father was up to. Whatever it was seemed to have the old man pretty stoked.

The trio followed him into the rundown barn.

The smell of hay, earth and manure filled Andrew's

nostrils as he eyed the old gray rafters overhead. The place looked a little better from the inside, but not by much. The roof was still shot.

Dad led them to one of the stalls, the wooden gate creaking when he opened it.

Megan gasped when she saw the two brand-new foals. "They're so *cute*."

"Easy, sweetie. We don't want to scare them." Carly kept her voice low and slipped an arm around her daughter's shoulders. "But they are adorable."

Andrew had to agree. The twins were chestnut colored, and each had a white blaze that stretched from the tops of their heads to their noses. It had been a long time since he'd seen a newborn anything.

"Where's their mother?" asked Carly.

Andrew suspected the answer but waited for his father to respond.

The old man coughed, his expression grim. "She had a tough time with the delivery."

Carly eyed him now, understanding lighting her baby blues. "So they're orphans?"

Dad nodded.

Andrew stepped closer and reached a hand into the pen to pet the soft fur of the first foal. "Remember when you and I used to help feed the calves way back when?" He looked at Carly now.

"How could I forget?" She moved beside him to pet the other foal. "They were so sweet, so little."

Megan looked perplexed. "Did you used to work here, Mommy?"

"No. But I used to hang out here a lot."

"How come?" Megan tilted her head, looking very serious.

Pink crept into Carly's cheeks. "I just liked being here."

"Your mama and Andrew used to be very good friends," said Dad.

Andrew caught his father's smirk before the old man went into another coughing fit. The sound was eerily familiar, reminding him of that summer Dad battled pneumonia. And how protective his mother had been from then on whenever he caught something as simple as a cold.

Urging Megan to pet the foal in his stead, Andrew moved toward his father. "Have you been to see a doctor about that cough?"

"I don't need no doctor. It's just a little chest cold." He leaned against the stall and changed the subject. "You know, these foals are going to require a lot of care and feedings. Unfortunately, time is one of those things I don't have a lot of."

"I can help, Clint," said Carly. "Matter of fact, I'd be happy to."

"Me, too." Megan bounced beside her mother.

Andrew wasn't sure how he felt about them spending time at the ranch. It reminded him too much of when he and Carly were dating. Ironically, some of his best memories were of their experiences together at the ranch.

"I thought I heard voices in here."

They all turned to greet his older brother, Noah. After years on the rodeo circuit, he now lived at the ranch and helped his father with the cattle, though his main focus was on the horses, as well as the trail rides and riding lessons they offered in the summer. Which made Andrew wonder…

"How come you've got the foals in here? I'd think you'd want them down at the stable."

"I asked him the same thing." Noah glared at the old man.

"And I told you, I want them close to the house." When

Dad looked Andrew's way, his eyes shimmered. "They were Chessie's babies."

Mama's horse. The one Dad had given her. Now Andrew understood.

While Dad went over the details of feeding the foals with Carly and Megan, Andrew took Noah aside. "How long has he been coughing like that?"

"A couple days, I guess."

Andrew mentally kicked himself for not paying closer attention. Just because he didn't like being at the ranch didn't give him an excuse to ignore his father. From now on, he'd have to keep a closer watch.

Chapter Nine

Carly breathed in the scents of the ranch as she made her way into the barn late Monday morning, armed with two feeding bottles. While some people might think the barnyard smells offensive, she found them rather comforting. Until Andrew brought her and Megan here on Friday, she'd never realized how much she missed the place.

During her high school years when she and Andrew dated, there were days when she spent more time at Abundant Blessings Ranch than she did at her own house. It was here that she'd learned how to fish and milk a cow, shimmy under a barbed wire fence without getting cut. And she was thrilled that her daughter would now get a chance to experience at least some of what the ranch had to offer. Abundant blessings indeed.

Too bad Andrew didn't feel that way about his own family home. She still didn't understand why he thought the place so abhorrent. Did he really believe the ranch had caused his mother's early death?

The babies were standing when she made it to their stall. One even tried to whinny, though it sounded more like a series of happy grunts.

"You guys know I've got food, don't you?" She swung open the gate and stepped inside the hay-covered space.

Immediately both foals nudged her hands with their velvety noses, eager to eat.

"Hold on a second." She positioned herself between them and lowered the bottles, one on each side of her.

Elsa and Anna—she still couldn't believe Clint had let Megan pick the babies' names—wasted no time latching on, behaving as though they hadn't eaten all day. In fact, this was their sixth feeding since midnight.

Noah and Andrew had taken turns, insisting their father sleep. The man's cough had grown increasingly disconcerting, and they'd also heard him wheezing. So, despite his father's objections, Andrew had taken him to the doctor.

She looked from one chestnut foal to the other. "You two need to slow down or you'll get a tummy ache."

While the twins continued to eat, she leaned against the wooden wall and contemplated all the crazy twists and turns her life had taken recently. Inheriting Livie's had meant she was one step closer to her dream coming true. But between Andrew's refusal to sell and the fire at Granger House, she'd once again been forced to relegate her dream to a back burner. Even if she could talk Andrew into selling, would she still be able to afford to buy him out?

After finally making it to the one-stop home improvement center late Friday, her eyes were opened to just how much everything was going to cost. Even little things like cup pulls and knobs for the kitchen cabinets, a sink, and pendant lights for over the island were more than she'd expected. Sure, she had good insurance, but that money would only go so far.

She let go a sigh, wondering why all of this was happening now. Was she not supposed to expand the bed-and-breakfast? Did God want her to keep taking in bookkeeping?

The thought made her cringe.

About the time Elsa and Anna finished draining their bottles, she heard the sound of gravel crunching under tires outside. That, coupled with the sound of a diesel engine, told her it was Andrew and his father.

She exited the stall, pausing to make sure the old latch was securely in place. "You girls take a nap. I'll be back later."

When she departed the barn, both father and son were getting out of the truck.

She shielded her eyes from the sun as Andrew tossed his door closed.

"So, what'd the doctor say?" Noah hollered as he jogged from the stable, his concern evident. He must have seen them drive up.

Andrew waited until they were all at the back of the truck. "He's got pneumonia. And he's been sentenced to bed rest."

"Oh." Her gaze drifted to the older man making his way up the steps, looking none too happy.

Noah shook his head. "He's not going to like that."

"Sputtered about it all the way home," said Andrew.

"Probably would have been better if they'd just put him in the hospital. I mean, what are we going to do?" Noah glanced from his brother to his father. "Hog-tie him?"

Andrew followed his brother's gaze. "I think we might have to hire someone to look after him. Besides, he wouldn't listen to us, anyway."

"That's silly." Tucking the two empty bottles under her arm, Carly brushed a windswept hair away from her face. "Why not just let me take care of him?"

Both brothers sent her the strangest look.

"At least during the day. I'm here helping with the foals anyway. And with Granger House out of commission, it's not like I have a whole lot to do."

She turned her attention solely to Andrew. "Besides, I want to help. Your family has always been so good to me, this is the least I can do."

"Are you sure you can handle him?" Noah's dark brow lifted. "He can be pretty stubborn, you know."

"I'm not worried." She watched the older man shuffle into the house. "Clint and I get along fine. He's a good man."

The brothers looked at each other as though sharing a silent conversation before turning back to her.

"Thank you, Carly," said Noah.

"If he gets to be too much, though," said Andrew, "you just let us know."

She smiled. "I will. But I doubt that'll be necessary." She took two steps toward the house, paused and turned back around. "Come on. I'll fix you guys some lunch."

After a quick meal of canned soup and roast beef sandwiches, Andrew headed back to town to work on Granger House, and Noah returned to his work in the stables. Clint settled into his recliner and willingly agreed to the breathing treatment the doctor had ordered. He fell asleep shortly thereafter, so she took the opportunity to sneak out and feed the foals.

When she returned, Clint was still sleeping, so since Andrew had offered to pick up Megan from school and bring her to the ranch, Carly pushed up her sleeves, ready to give the ranch house some much-needed TLC. The Stephens men weren't necessarily messy, but there was something to be said for a good, thorough cleaning. Especially in the kitchen.

She cleared the off-white Formica countertops of clutter before scrubbing them down with bleach, along with the sink and stove. Next she cleaned out the refrigerator, wiped it down, then grabbed a package of chicken from the freezer. All the while, she'd periodically poke her head around the corner to check on Clint, pleased to see he was still asleep. Rest was exactly what he needed to get better.

While the meat thawed in the microwave, she searched the cupboards, trying to figure out what she could make the guys for dinner. Their pantry didn't have a whole lot of variety. Canned soup and veggies, some tomato sauce, pasta… A casserole, perhaps.

Inspired, she put the chicken on to boil. No sooner had she set the lid atop the pot when the sound of Clint's raspy breathing drew her into the adjoining family room. He was awake now, his forest-green recliner upright, and he was looking a bit pale.

"How are you feeling?" She knelt beside his chair, resting a hand on his forearm.

"I know my boys asked you to stay here. But there's no need to fuss over me, young lady. I've been taking care of myself for a long time."

She bit back a laugh. While Clint Stephens might indeed be capable of taking care of himself, his wife, Mona, was the kind of woman who went above and beyond when it came to her men. Tough when she had to be, but not afraid to spoil them, either. Something Carly had always admired.

"I understand. I'm pretty good at taking care of myself, too. But everyone needs a little help now and then. If it hadn't been for Andrew and other folks around town, I never would have made it through these last couple of weeks." She patted his arm. "Now, what can I get you?"

He clasped his hands over his trim belly. "I reckon I could use a cup of coffee."

She was thinking more along the lines of juice or tea.

"I like it black. And strong." A man's man through and through.

"Coming right up." She pushed to her feet. "And just for the record, Andrew and Noah did not ask me to stay with you. I volunteered."

The older man seemed a little more amicable after that. He turned on the television situated in the corner of the room and watched some police show while she assembled the chicken spaghetti casserole. She put the pan in the oven and washed her hands before going to check on him again.

His chair was empty.

"Clint?" Her gaze darted around the room. She checked the hall to see if perhaps he'd gone to the restroom. Then she heard sounds coming from the mudroom.

She entered to find the man wearing his coat and hat and heading out the door.

Suddenly grateful for being a little on the small side, she darted around him to block the opening. "Just where do you think you're going?"

"I have a ranch to tend to."

"Not under my watch, you don't." She held her ground. Even when he closed what little distance there was between them, to tower over her. Though she had no doubt he could push right past her if he really wanted to. She could only hope that—

"Young lady, I suggest you get out of my way." Determined dark eyes bored into hers.

But she had no intention of letting Andrew and Noah down. One way or another, she would win this battle.

Clouds gathered over the mountains to the west as Andrew's pickup bumped over the cattle guard at the entrance to Abundant Blessings. He couldn't remember ever being this eager to get to the ranch. Not that it was the ranch spurring him on. Instead, he was worried about his father.

Why had it taken him so long to notice Dad's cough? If he hadn't been there, would Noah have picked up on it? He didn't want to cast stones at his brother, but what if Andrew hadn't been in town? Suppose Dad had gotten sick and Noah hadn't realized it until it was too late?

What if his father had been at the end and Andrew didn't get a chance to say goodbye?

Truth be told, that was the part that had bothered him all afternoon. What if something happened to his father and he wasn't there? What if he never got to say goodbye?

He drew in a deep breath, refusing to let that scenario play out again.

Then there was Carly. He and Noah had practically dumped the old man on her. It wasn't her responsibility to take care of him. No, either he or Noah should have stayed with their father until they could hire someone.

"I hope Mommy hasn't fed the foals yet." Megan's words as she squirmed in the passenger seat pulled him out of his thoughts. She was every bit as impatient as he was to get to the ranch, albeit for different reasons.

"Are you kidding?" He glanced her way. "You saw how much they ate this weekend. Even if she did feed them, they'll be ready to go again in no time."

She giggled. "Yeah, they were *really* hungry."

Since both Noah's and Dad's trucks were parked close to the house, he pulled up to the far end of the deck. He shifted into Park, his gaze suddenly drawn to the entrance to the mudroom. Why was Carly standing in the open doorway? And why was her stance so rigid, her arms crossed?

Beyond her, he glimpsed his father. Cowboy hat atop his head, he glared down at Carly, looking fit to be tied.

Andrew's heart twisted. How could he have been so naive? He should have known better than to leave her alone with the old man. Clint Stephens was as stubborn as they came. No one except his wife had ever tangled with him and come out a winner. And from the looks of things, Dad had every intention of winning the battle of wills brewing between him and Carly.

Andrew exited the truck and grabbed Megan, tucking her behind him as they climbed the three steps onto the deck.

"Clint Stephens, you get back in that recliner right now or I'll have Noah and Andrew here so fast it'll make your head spin." Apparently neither Carly nor his father had noticed them.

A bone-chilling breeze kicked up as he moved beside the house, lifting the collar on his jacket. Looking down at Megan, he touched a finger to his lips.

Eyes wide, she nodded, seemingly understanding his silent request.

Peering around the corner, he continued to watch. A part of him was ready to rush to Carly's side and give his father a piece of his mind. But the other, more rational part told him to stay put and let her handle things. Because despite his father's intimidation tactics, she was doing a good job of holding her own. Much like his mother had done.

The thought made him smile.

His father continued to stare Carly down, but she wasn't budging. Dad started coughing then, his body convulsing. The cold air must have gotten to him.

Showing no mercy, Carly said, "You might think you're ready to go out there, but your body is telling you otherwise."

The old man continued to cough.

She stood her ground, though. "You gonna be stubborn

and ignore it? Or are you man enough to listen to what your body is trying to tell you?"

Andrew had to smother his laugh. She had his dad's number, all right.

His father removed his hat and turned around.

"Okay, then." Carly's posture eased. "Let's get you settled." She stepped away from the door, closing it behind her. She'd obviously won the battle of wills. Just like his mama.

He breathed a sigh of relief, another thought niggling his brain. He'd underestimated Carly. Not to mention his father. It irked him to no end to think that his father had tried to bully her.

He glanced back at Megan. "Your mama's one tough cookie, you know that?"

The kid grinned. "Can we go see the foals now?"

"Sure."

The foals attempted to nicker as he and Megan made their way into the barn. He pushed the door closed, glad that the dilapidated structure still blocked the wind.

While Megan petted and talked baby talk to Elsa and Anna, he tried to wrap his brain around the wayward thoughts that were suddenly bombarding him. Until now, he'd always thought of Carly as the girl he once loved. But seeing the tough yet tender way she dealt with his father had him realizing she'd become an amazing woman.

"I thought I saw you two sneaking in here." Noah closed the door, armed with two bottles. "Megan, you think those babies are hungry again?"

She nodded, her smile morphing into a giggle as one of the foals nuzzled her neck.

Grinning, Noah handed her one of the bottles. "Looks like we'd better hurry before they decide to make a snack out of you."

"Have you been in the house yet?" Leaning against the side of the stall, Noah offered the second bottle to Elsa.

Andrew shook his head. "No. Though we did witness an interesting exchange between Carly and the old man."

His brother's eyes narrowed. "How so?"

Andrew explained what had transpired.

"Maybe Carly isn't the right person to watch Dad, after all."

"Are you kidding? She's perfect," said Andrew. "I mean, when was the last time you were able to get the old man to back down?"

"Good point."

"Besides, Carly volunteered. It's not like we coerced her or anything."

"True."

"I talked to Jude. He's working a double shift today but should be in tonight."

"That's good. I'm going to need him to help me with the cattle." Noah smirked. "That is, unless you'd like to help me."

Andrew held his hands up. "Don't look at me. I've got plenty to do at Granger House."

"Excuses, excuses." His big brother dragged the toe of his well-worn boot through the dirt. "I called Matt."

Their middle brother and Dad had always had a volatile relationship, but even more so after Mom passed away. She was the glue that had kept things together. Without her... "How did that go?"

Noah shrugged. "You know Matt. He doesn't say much. Just that things are busy at the Sheriff's department, but he might stop by." They shared a knowing look, neither believing that Matt would actually show.

"What about Daniel?" Their baby brother was the adventurer of the family and currently white-water rafting in South America. "You need me to contact him?"

"Nah, I'll email him tonight, let him know what's going on. It's not like he can do anything anyway." Noah pushed off from the wall. "Mind taking over for me? I need to run back up to the stable."

The two traded places.

"Guess I'll see you at supper," said Noah on his way to the door.

"Who's cooking? You or me?"

One side of his brother's mouth lifted. "Neither. I checked in with Carly earlier. Said she's got us covered."

When the foals finished eating, Andrew and Megan made their way to the house. Stepping inside, he was overcome with the most incredible aromas. Food the likes of which this house hadn't known since his mother's passing.

Moving from the mudroom into the main part of the house, he was taken aback. His father was in his recliner with a plastic mask over his mouth, looking very pale.

Beside him, Carly turned off the machine that provided the breathing treatments. "Feel better now?"

Dad nodded and removed the mask, his hesitant gaze drifting to Carly's. "Thank you."

Andrew almost fell over. If he hadn't heard it for himself, he never would have believed it. Carly had definitely won the old man over.

And Andrew couldn't say he blamed him.

Chapter Ten

By midday Tuesday, Carly had cleaned just about everything she could clean at the ranch house. She fixed herself another cup of tea, scooped up the mug and leaned against the pristine counter, watching Clint sleep in his recliner. His continued wheezing was cause for concern. She'd hoped there would be some sign of improvement, yet things were, perhaps, even a little worse. Then again, it had been only twenty-four hours. She prayed he might turn a corner tomorrow. In the meantime, she'd do her best to keep him comfortable, well rested and nourished.

The timer she'd set on her phone vibrated in her back pocket since she didn't want to risk waking him.

She set her cup on the counter and turned off the timer before retrieving two large baking sheets of oatmeal raisin cookies from the oven. Chocolate chip had been her first choice, but since there were no chocolate chips to be found at the ranch house… Maybe she'd pick some up for tomorrow.

Spatula in hand, she transferred the cookies to the cooling racks she'd laid out on the long wooden table. It felt good to cook for other people again. That's one of the things she missed the most about Granger House Inn being out of commission.

She was off the hook for tonight's dinner, though. Rose Daniels had gotten wind of Clint's illness and called Carly earlier, wanting to know how the townspeople could help.

Carly had thanked her and then, as tactfully as she could, went on to express her concerns about Clint's health and potentially exposing him or any visitors to unwanted germs. To which Rose replied, "You're right, dear. I'll just let everyone know that the Stephens have got you to cook for them, so no meals are needed." And then the woman promptly volunteered to bring them some pulled pork for tonight.

Setting the empty baking pans in the sink, Carly chuckled. She could only hope to have a heart as big as Rose Daniels's.

After washing the baking sheets and moving the cooled cookies to a storage container, she glanced around the room. Surely there was something productive she could do. She wasn't one simply to sit and twiddle her thumbs. Maybe she should start bringing her laptop so she could knock out some bookkeeping while Clint was asleep.

Cup in hand, she wandered down the hallway to see if she'd missed anything. She'd washed Clint's sheets as well as dusted and vacuumed his room but had vowed not to enter any of the brothers' rooms. Noah had moved back in after leaving the rodeo circuit a few years back; Jude still spent much of his time here, helping his father with cattle; and Daniel kept his room for the rare occasion he wasn't traveling. Which he was currently doing, so Andrew was occupying the space.

Continuing to drift, she entered the small room that had been Mona's crafting space. Spools of colorful ribbon still hung from dowels attached to the wall, while decorative papers and fabric had been tossed into baskets and boxes and pushed against the walls, as though someone had cleaned up the space without really knowing where things went.

On the far side of the room, a long countertop stretched the length of the wall with shoe boxes and a stack of books piled in one corner. Moving across the worn beige carpet, she realized that they were scrapbooks. She set her cup down and lifted the cover on the top one. The first page was blank, as were the second and third pages. They all were.

Perplexed, she closed the scrapbook, set it aside and reached for the next one. Also empty. Three, four and five, too. Hmph.

Picking up her tea, she took another sip. Maybe they were just extras.

As she lowered the cup, her gaze fell to the boxes beside the scrapbooks. Just regular old shoe bo—

What was that?

She leaned in for a closer look at the one on top. There was a handwritten *N* in one corner.

Returning her mug to the counter, she tugged the box toward her, casting a glance over her shoulder to make sure no one was coming. She had no business doing this. These could be Mona's most cherished possessions. Yet something compelled her to look.

With the first box in front of her, she glimpsed the corners of the second box, finally spotting an *A*. Nudging it aside, she moved on to the third box. Sure enough, there was an *M* on one of its corners.

She grabbed the box with the *A*, set it atop the one already in front of her and lifted the lid to discover dozens of photos. A smile played on her lips at the sight of a baby Andrew staring up at her. All that dark hair. Simply adorable.

Picking up the photo, she turned it over. It was labeled Andrew—4 months old.

As she continued to look through the box, she saw that some photos had been grouped together. Each bundle was tied with ribbon and had a slip of paper tucked on the top, describing what the photos were about. Labels such as Andrew—Ranch Photos, Andrew—Scouts... In addition, every picture had extensive notes written on the back.

She returned Andrew's photos to the appropriate box before checking the other four. Each was organized in the exact same manner, and there was a separate box for each of Mona's five boys.

Carly could only imagine the time this must have taken. Talk about a labor of love. But that was so like Mona.

She glanced at the empty scrapbooks. Five scrapbooks, five boxes. Had Mona intended to put together a scrapbook for each of her sons?

Except her plans never came to fruition. Carly leaned against the counter. Could she pick up where Mona left off?

She quickly put everything away, tucking it all back the way she had found it, and returned to the family room with a renewed sense of purpose.

Later, after Clint woke up and had accepted another breathing treatment, she brought him some cookies, settled on the overstuffed loveseat next to him and told him what she had found.

"That's all she did during those last months." Clint leaned back in his recliner. "All she could do, really. She always liked to give the boys something sentimental at Christmas. Those scrapbooks were supposed to be their gift that year." His voice cracked. "The cancer got her before she could make them, though."

Carly battled her own emotions, covering by retreating to the kitchen to get him some more juice.

When she returned, she set the glass on the table beside him before taking her seat again. "What would you think about me completing the scrapbooks in Mona's stead?"

"No." He shook his head. "It wouldn't be the same."

"I'm afraid I'd have to disagree." She stood and started toward the hallway.

"Where are you going?"

"You'll see." Determined to overcome his objection, she grabbed Andrew's box and brought it to his father. Opening it up, she said, "Just look at how orderly and detailed Mona left everything. As though she were hoping someone would pick up where she left off."

Tears filled the older man's dark eyes as he fingered his wife's handwritten notes. "She did all this?" He sniffed and continued to dig through the box.

After examining the contents, he looked over at Carly. "You might be right." He placed the lid back on the box and handed it to her. "It would be a shame to let all of my wife's hard work go to waste." He smiled then, his cheeks wet with tears. "I believe she would be very appreciative if you completed this project that was so near to her heart."

"I would be honored to do it, Clint."

He dabbed his eyes with a napkin before reclining again. "I know I haven't been the easiest patient, but I thank you for taking care of me, Carly."

She smiled, grateful that they'd managed to come to an understanding yesterday.

"And for giving Andrew a reason to hang around a while, though I'm sorry it had to be at your expense."

She blinked away the tears that threatened. "Believe

it or not, Clint, your sons still need you. Which is precisely why you need to get well."

Things were looking up by Wednesday afternoon. At least in Andrew's mind. His father was doing better, Carly's new windows and door had been installed, and Marianne had called from the design studio to say that the cabinets would be shipped sooner than expected.

Now, as he made his way to the ranch with Megan, his mind was reeling. Since the timeline had been bumped up, he needed decisions from Carly. Namely appliances. They'd looked at tons of them this past weekend, but aside from the special-order commercial range, Carly was still mulling things over. The time had arrived to make those purchases.

Walking into the ranch house, he was again greeted with the smells of home. An aromatic dinner and a hint of something sweet. He could get used to coming home to Carly. A beautiful woman, great company, fantastic cook…

While Megan went on inside, he paused in the mudroom, confused by the train of thought his mind had taken. After all, he'd soon be headed back to Denver to embark on the next phase of his life. And Carly would never leave the life she'd built for her and her daughter.

He gave himself a stern shake before meeting her in the kitchen. "Good news. Your cabinets are arriving early." He followed her from the stove to the refrigerator. "So we need to get your appliances on order ASAP."

Carly poured a short glass of milk and put three snickerdoodles on a plate. "Sorry, but I can't think about the kitchen right now." She crossed to the table and set both in front of Megan and her homework. The woman was like a well-oiled machine.

She faced him now. Worry puckered her brow as she shoved the sleeves of her black sweater to her elbows. "Your father's fever is up."

"What?" The old man seemed to be doing so well this morning. How could things change so quickly?

"I've already contacted the doctor. Trent's going to drop by on his way home, possibly give him a shot of antibiotics." She heaved a sigh. "If that doesn't work, he's going to the hospital."

Andrew's heart skidded to a halt. "But… I thought he was doing better." He eyed his dad in the recliner, thanking God that he was in Ouray and not Denver. Though if he were, he'd have come immediately. He'd learned that lesson the hard way. Still, what if he lost his dad? What would he do? They were getting on so well.

No, he wouldn't let anything happen. He couldn't.

He watched as Carly went to his father, touched a hand to his cheek, then returned to the kitchen with his empty glass.

"Why isn't he in bed?" Andrew practically barked out the words as Carly returned to the kitchen.

Carly's blue eyes narrowed. "Because he refused. If he's more comfortable in his chair, then let him be in his chair." She glanced at the empty glass in her hand. "I need to get him some more juice."

"I'll get it." Andrew took the cup from her and headed to the fridge for some apple juice. His hands were shaking as he tipped the carton. He bumped the glass, spilling the juice all over the linoleum floor.

He let out a frustrated growl.

Next thing he knew, Carly was at his side. She laid a hand on his arm and smiled up at him, as if understanding more than just his frustration over the juice. "I've got this." Taking hold of the glass, she turned to her daughter. "Megan, why don't you take Andrew out to feed the foals? I think he could use some fresh air."

He hated to leave. Still, he knew Carly was right. He'd thought things were on the upswing. Now he needed to come to terms with this latest turn of events. Apparently Carly knew him better than he thought. Not that that was anything new.

While he and Megan fed the foals, he raked a hand through his hair and stared at the holes in the ancient roof. Dad was only sixty-five. Too young to die. He should have been enjoying retirement, not spending all his time worrying about this stupid ranch.

God, why is this happening? First Mama then Grandma... Are You ready to take Dad, too?

Lowering his gaze, he shook his head from side to side. Who was he to be questioning God?

Nobody, that's who. He had no power. He didn't cause the sun to rise and set. He didn't tell the rain and snow to fall from their storehouses.

No, he was a mere man. One who often failed to recognize that he wasn't in charge. That he didn't always get his way. Life was always changing. And not always according to his plan, amplifying the conviction that his job was simply to have faith. Even when he didn't understand.

When the doctor arrived a short time later, Andrew, Megan and Noah joined everyone inside. The doctor gave Dad a shot of antibiotics, along with instructions for Carly to call tomorrow with an update on his progress.

Andrew walked him out. "Thank you for coming out, Dr. Lockridge."

"No thanks necessary. I pass right by here on my way home." He reached for the door of his truck. "And call me Trent."

Andrew nodded. "Thanks, Trent."

Between the doctor's visit and a dinner of homemade chicken noodle soup, Andrew's mood was much improved. Then again, that was the kind of meal that was therapeutic on so many different levels. Throw in a few snickerdoodles and he happily agreed to take care of the dishes while Carly gave his father another breathing treatment.

The fact that she'd stayed so late said a lot about her concern for his father. It was a school night, after all, and Megan would need to get to bed soon.

When Andrew and Noah finally convinced her that they'd take turns monitoring their father, Carly donned her coat, telling Megan to go say good-night to the foals.

The cold night air fell around them as Andrew walked her to her SUV. He eyed the starry sky. "They're saying we might be in for a snowstorm."

"Not surprising. It is only March, you know." Stopping beside the vehicle, she shoved her hands in the pockets of her fleece jacket and looked up at him. "How are you doing?"

"Better, thanks to you."

"I didn't do so much. It's Trent who saved the day."

He couldn't argue that. Just knowing he was willing to stop by after hours meant a lot. Thanks to him, Dad was resting comfortably and, Lord willing, the shot would have him feeling better tomorrow.

He dragged his fingers through his hair. "I sure hope so."

As he lowered his hand, she took hold of it. "I know you're scared."

His eyes searched hers, a weight settling in the pit of his stomach. She knew him too well. But did she have any idea just how scared he was? Did she understand why? Did she know that he'd ignored Noah's repeated pleas for him to come and allowed himself to become so busy that he wasn't even there when his mother died?

Then, as if reading his thoughts, she dropped his hand and wrapped her arms around his neck. "You're a good man, Andrew. And a good son." She kissed his cheek before letting go. "Megan, come on, sweetie. Time to go."

A flurry of emotions swirled through him as he watched her drive away. He was grateful God had brought her back into his life. Because with Carly around, he suddenly didn't feel so alone.

Chapter Eleven

Talk about a dilemma.

Carly awoke the next morning, eager to get to the ranch to check on Clint. Yet not quite as eager to see Andrew. Why on earth had she hugged him last night? That made twice in recent weeks she'd allowed herself to get caught up in her emotions. This time she'd even kissed him. On the cheek, but still... When he'd had the opportunity to kiss her that night at Livie's after she'd dropped the plate, he hadn't taken the chance.

To make matters worse, when she did arrive at the ranch shortly after dropping Megan off at school, he'd barely said goodbye before he was out the door. As if he couldn't bear to face her.

Fine by her. She was feeling a little sheepish herself. Obviously Andrew's only interest in her was as a friend, client and caretaker for his father. As it should be. So why did it bother her so much?

At least she could take heart in the fact that Clint was doing better. She'd prayed all night that he would show some sign of improvement by this morning, and from what she could tell, he was. He had more color and seemed to be more alert. Best of all, his fever was down.

Now it was up to her to make sure it stayed that way. Forward progress was good. Going backward wasn't. She couldn't let her guard down with either Clint or Andrew.

As for Clint, she'd have to monitor his temperature, bump up the number of breathing treatments, and make sure he got the fluids and rest he needed. Whatever it took to keep him out of the hospital.

"It's downright freezing out there today." Eyeing Clint, she added two more split logs to the wood-burning stove that kept the common areas of the house nice and toasty. "And from the looks of those clouds—" she nodded toward the picture window "—we might be in for a little snow, too."

"Glad I don't have to worry about going out there, then." Clint burrowed deeper into his recliner, adjusting the blanket over his legs. A hint, perhaps, that he still had a long road to recovery.

"No, you do not." She closed the glass doors on the stove, smiling, then slipped her hands into the back pockets of her jeans as she straightened. "The only thing you have to worry about is getting well. So you just relax and take it easy."

She retrieved the remote from the arm of the couch and punched in the numbers for Clint's favorite channel. The one that played all the old Westerns.

Seeing the cowboy-hat-clad hero that appeared on the screen, she couldn't help noticing how similar his attire was to Clint's when he was working the ranch. Then it dawned on her. These were the shows Clint would have watched as a kid growing up in Ouray. No wonder he'd wanted to become a rancher. She could only imagine the childhood dreams he'd fulfilled since he and Mona bought the land that was Abundant Blessings Ranch all those years ago. They'd been partners in every sense of the word. Something Carly admired.

Her parents had been the same way about Granger House Inn. So when they passed it on to her, she'd envisioned Dennis and her fulfilling the same role. But his interest in the B and B was limited to income. Everything else seemed to fall on her.

Not much of a partnership.

Now, as she finished cleaning up the kitchen from breakfast, Clint was asleep, so she took the opportunity to head into Mona's craft room to start working on the scrapbooks. Every time she so much as thought about them, she got excited.

Talk about an awesome responsibility. Thankfully, Mona had all of the details written out. Even so far as to state how the pictures were to be arranged.

Standing at the long counter with the first blank scrapbook open, she took a deep breath and lifted the lid on Noah's box of photos. Such a cute baby. Though, truthfully, the Stephens boys all kind of looked the same. Dark hair, dark eyes…until you got to Daniel. Blond, blue-eyed…a complete departure from the rest of them. That boy definitely favored his mama.

Once she had removed all of the photos from the box, she noticed the colorful papers and cutouts used for scrapbooking tucked in the bottom. She picked up a small envelope and found that it was unsealed. More instructions, perhaps?

She pulled out the note card adorned with Colorado columbines, opened it and read.

My dearest Noah…

Carly covered her mouth with her hand, a lump forming in her throat. Mona had even written them letters… when she knew she was dying.

The first time I held you in my arms, I knew I was created to be a mother. You were my sunshine on cloudy days, always quick with a smile. But that smile faded when Jaycee died—

Carly blinked away tears. Noah had lost his wife when she developed an infection after miscarrying their first child. And a grieving Noah returned to the rodeo circuit, as though daring God to take him, too.

Closing the card, she tucked it back into its envelope. It wasn't hers to read. Though she was more determined than ever to complete this task.

Lord, thank You for allowing me to find these boxes. Please guide me and help me bring Mona's vision to life for her boys—

Uh-oh. Voices echoed from the main part of the house. Andrew. Noah.

Drat. She must have lost track of time. Was it lunchtime already?

She scrambled to put everything back into the box, praying neither of the brothers would find her and spoil this magnificent surprise.

Shoving the box alongside the others, she hurried down the hall, pausing to take a deep breath before rounding into the family room. Sure was a lot of commotion going on. Didn't they realize they were going to wake Clint?

When she continued into the family room, she saw Noah adding more wood to the already more-than-sufficient stack along one wall and Andrew hauling in multiple bags of groceries. Surely this wasn't the end of the world.

"Looks like you guys are preparing for the worst." She crossed to the kitchen, where Andrew had begun unloading everything from pantry staples to milk, eggs, meats and cheeses. "It's just a little snow."

They looked at each other before Noah addressed her. Something that was really starting to bug her. If they had something to say— "Storm's moving in quicker than expected."

Andrew pulled two boxes of cereal from one bag. "And a Pacific disturbance is giving it lots of fuel."

Okay, even she knew that wasn't good. After all, she'd lived her entire life in Ouray.

Arms empty, Noah moved toward her. "We're under a blizzard warning from this evening until tomorrow or the next day."

"I had no idea." She should have paid closer attention to the weather this morning. Because if this came to fruition, keeping both Clint and the foals safe would be a challenge. Particularly if the electricity went out. She just hoped the guys were up to the challenge. "I guess I'd better plan to leave early today so I can pick up Megan. We'll have to hunker down at Livie's."

"Actually…" Andrew came alongside her then. So close she could feel the warmth radiating from his body. Though that was nothing compared to the warmth she saw in his coffee-colored eyes. "I'd feel better if the two of you stayed here."

Did he really think her that helpless? Or did he simply want her here to take care of Clint? Well, he was a big boy and *she'd* been taking care of herself and Megan for a long time, so she didn't need—

"I need to know that you and Megan are safe." He caressed her cheek with the back of his hand, rendering her virtually speechless.

There wasn't a thing she could do except swallow the lump in her throat, look up at him and manage to say, "Okay."

By the time Carly served up a hearty dinner of beef stew and homemade bread, the wind had really kicked up and snow had begun to fall, right along with the temperature. Now, as Andrew burrowed deeper under the quilt his grandmother had made, the winds howled, rattling the bedroom windows.

Staring at the blue numbers on the alarm clock, he was surprised that the electricity had stayed on past midnight. Typically they would have been plunged into darkness by now. At least until someone fired up the generator.

He breathed a sigh of relief that Carly and Megan were here, safely down the hall in Jude's room. Since his policeman brother was needed in town, he'd opted to stay at Matt's. Even if he hadn't, though, Andrew would have gladly given up his room—well, Daniel's room—and slept on the couch. Whatever it took to make sure that Carly and Megan were comfortable and taken care of.

A loud crack sounded from outside, sending Andrew bolting from his bed. More cracking, followed by a crash.

Confused, he lifted the blinds on the window and looked outside, but the snow was coming down too heavy to see anything else.

A million scenarios ran through his mind as he rushed from the room.

Noah was already in the mudroom, coat in hand.

"What was that?" Andrew asked his brother.

"I have no idea, but I intend to find out."

Andrew grabbed his own coat, put that over the Henley and sweatpants he'd worn to bed and shoved his feet into his boots, the actions reminding him of when they were kids. Always wanting to keep up with his big brother. "I'm coming with you."

Outside, the snow was coming down sideways, propelled by the force of the wind. Even with the floodlights, it was nearly impossible to see.

Noah looked left, then right. "We'd better check the barn." He had to yell to be heard over the wind.

Andrew followed him through the snow. "What's that noise?" There was something else besides the wind. Something…alive.

Noah stopped in front of him. Turned his head. "I hear it, too."

Andrew squinted, trying hard to see past all of the white.

Suddenly his eyes widened. "The barn!" Or rather, what was left of it.

"The foals!" Noah darted ahead.

Andrew was on his heels. Drawing closer, he could see that the entire section where the foals were had caved in. But they were still alive. That was the sound he heard.

Together, he and his big brother examined the collapse, trying to determine where the horses were and how to get to them.

"I'll be right back." Andrew sprinted to his truck for some flashlights. Once he returned, it didn't take long to find the animals. Unfortunately, they were wedged between the wall that still stood and a large amount of debris. And they were too spooked to come out on their own.

Noah ducked under the wreckage in an effort to reach them.

"Andrew!"

He turned at the sound of Carly's voice. "What are you doing out here? Get back—"

She put one booted foot in front of the other, her eyes widening. "The foals? Are they—?"

"No." Noah emerged from the rubble then. "But they're trapped."

"Where?" Beside Andrew now, she stooped to look.

Both men shone their flashlights, the snow pelting their faces.

"That timber—" Noah motioned with his light "—is holding things up." Lowering the beam, he looked at Carly. "It's also preventing me from getting to them. I can't get past it. I'm too big."

"I'm not."

Andrew recognized the expression of determination on her pretty face.

He looked at his brother, his heart constricting. With this kind of wind, it was only a matter of time before that timber went down, too. And when it did, the foals would likely be crushed. So the thought of sending Carly in there didn't settle well.

Noah stared at him as if waiting for Andrew's approval.

Carly clutched his arm. "We can't let them die."

He knew that. Didn't mean he had to like it, though.

He met her gaze now. "You'd better be careful. Things could topple at any second."

"I will." A hint of trepidation puckered her brow. "I promise."

Andrew and Noah kept their flashlights aimed on the foals, providing as much light as possible for Carly as she made her way into the barn.

Andrew's heart wrenched, his breath hanging in his throat. *God, please keep her safe—*

Before his prayer was finished, she had shimmied under the timber, all the while talking to the foals. Coaxing them.

How she managed to keep a soothing tone to her voice amid this chaos was beyond him.

One horse tentatively moved toward her, then the other.

"Come on, babies." Beside him, his brother cheered them on, though not loudly enough to scare them.

A few seconds later, Carly managed to slip behind the foals and urge them to safety.

"Better get ready to grab one." Noah positioned himself in front of the opening.

Elsa came out first, and Noah scooped her into his arms.

Andrew moved into place and duplicated his brother's move with Anna.

Suddenly, a loud crack ripped through the air.

"Carly!"

The timber had given way.

She was just about out when boards and shingles began raining down on her. She covered her head with her hands and arms. Then she went down.

He started to put the horse down, but she saw him.

"No!" Lying on her stomach, she struggled to break free. "I'm okay." A grimace belied her words. She grunted. "I'm just stuck."

He couldn't bear the thought of leaving her.

"Andrew?"

Over the raging wind, he looked at her again.

Her blue eyes pleaded with him. "Go!"

Noah nudged his arm. "Let's get them to the stable."

The stable? Carrying a hundred-pound weight? That would take forever. But with no bridle or rope to lead them, he held the foal tight and made his way to the stable as quickly as possible, willing God to propel his every step.

Once the horses were settled into a stall, he left Noah

to take care of them and rushed back out into the blinding snow.

He ran as fast as he could. His lungs were burning, his face numb despite the sweat that beaded his brow, but it didn't matter. Carly was all he cared about.

Anger burned in his gut. Dad had no business keeping those animals in that decrepit barn. Even after Noah had suggested they move them for the duration of the storm, the old man insisted they remain near the house. Now Carly might have to pay for his foolishness with her life.

Approaching the barn, he skidded to a halt. Through almost whiteout conditions, he saw his father pulling Carly from the rubble.

Somehow she managed to stand, but she was limping. Andrew rushed to help.

"I'm fine," she said. "My ankle was caught, that's all. Just get me inside."

Megan met them at the door, her blue eyes wider than he'd ever seen. "Mommy? Are you okay?"

"I'm fine, baby." She hugged her daughter.

"What about the foals?" Megan fretted. "Are they okay?"

"Yes, they are." Andrew dusted the snow from his hair. "They're in the stable with Noah."

"That's a good girl you've got there, Carly." His father patted Megan on the back. "Stayed put, just like I asked her to."

Andrew felt his nostrils flare. "The foals should have been kept in the stable to begin with. It's safer, more secure…"

His father's gaze momentarily narrowed before he began to cough.

"Andrew, I need you to stoke the fire for me, please." Carly's expression told him she was none too happy with him for calling his father out. He didn't care, though. It needed to be said. He'd seen enough pain and suffering here at the ranch to know that there was no room for poor choices.

He dutifully tended the fire while Carly helped the old man to his chair.

"I think it would be wise to do another breathing treatment." She reached for the nebulizer.

"Oh, if I have to," the old man wheezed.

"Yes, you have to. But what do you say I reward you with some hot cocoa when you're done?"

Hands clasped in his lap, the old man gave a weak smile. "I'd say things are looking up. Care to join me, Megan?"

"For cocoa? Oh, yeah."

With his father settled, Carly headed into the kitchen.

Andrew followed, noting there was still a slight hitch in her step. Her ankle had to be killing her. She shouldn't even be on her feet. "You're sure you're okay?"

She pulled the milk from the fridge. "I'm fine. I just needed a little help getting out from under all that weight." At the stove, she poured the milk into a pan. Added some sugar, cocoa and cinnamon.

He came up behind her, laying a hand against the small of her back. "You know, if it hadn't been for you, those foals would have been crushed."

She continued to whisk the mixture as though trying to ignore him. "I'm just glad they listened to me."

He tucked her damp curls behind her ear. "You're their mama. They know your voice."

She peered up at him now, her tremulous smile warming him from the inside out.

What would he have done if something had happened

to her? Because if there was one thing tonight had shown him for sure, it was that his feelings for Carly had moved far beyond friendship.

Chapter Twelve

Carly opened her eyes several hours later and stared into the predawn darkness of Andrew's brother's bedroom. Beside her, Megan's even breathing confirmed that she was still sound asleep. No wonder, with all the excitement they'd had last night. Or rather, earlier this morning.

Unfortunately, excitement was becoming all too familiar to Carly. The last two weeks of her life had hovered somewhere between a nightmare and a dream. First the fire, then planning the perfect kitchen, caring for Clint and spending time with Andrew. Time that had involved a plethora of emotions, everything from fear to bliss. Andrew made her feel things she hadn't felt in forever. Things she'd vowed never to feel again.

So, as she eased out from under the covers now, careful not to disturb her daughter, she couldn't help wondering what might be in store for her today.

The freezing-cold air sent a shiver down her spine as she tugged her bulky cable-knit sweater over the base layer she'd slept in. The electricity must have finally fallen prey to the storm. Fortunately, when she'd picked up Megan from school yesterday, they'd had time to stop by Livie's to grab some toiletries and extra clothing.

Stepping into her jeans, she was pleased to discover that the ankle caught in the collapse no longer bothered her. Curious, she put all of her weight onto it.

No pain at all.

When the barn came crashing down on her, she'd feared the worst. Instead, God had protected her and the foals.

She eased into the chair beside the door, sending up a prayer of thanks as she shoved her feet into a pair of fuzzy socks. She also lifted up her concerns for Clint, praying that being out in the wind and freezing temps last night hadn't set back his recovery. The man needed to be healthy again so he could return to doing the things he loved so much. Such as tending this ranch.

With that in mind, it appeared her mission for today was clear. To see to it that the Stephens men and Megan were taken care of. This blessed assignment had filled that void left by the B and B, giving her purpose once again. One far better than bookkeeping.

Emerging from the bedroom, she softly closed the door behind her so as not to wake Megan and padded silently down the hall.

The faintest hint of light appeared through the picture window in the family room while flames danced behind the glass doors of the wood-burning stove, as though someone had recently stoked the fire. And the aroma of fresh-brewed coffee filled the air.

"Good morning." The sound of Andrew's voice sent her heart aflutter.

Rubbing her arms, she turned to see his silhouette approaching from the kitchen. "Morning."

"Noah went out to fire up the generator." Andrew stopped in front of her now, coffee mug in hand, the soft glow from the fire illuminating his amazing eyes. "So we should have some lights soon."

"Lights are good." But she was more interested in heat. She moved closer to the stove. At least it was warmer out here than in the bedroom.

Then she noticed Clint's empty recliner. She prayed that he was warm enough in his room and that he was sleeping well.

Turning, Andrew went back to the kitchen. "How's the foot?" He opened one cupboard, then another, though it was difficult to make out what he was doing.

"Believe it or not, it doesn't hurt at all."

"Really?" He continued whatever it was he was doing. "That's good." A minute later he returned to her side with a second mug. "One English breakfast tea."

"Thank you." She took hold of the cup with both hands, savoring the warmth from both the tea and the gesture. She liked the way Andrew anticipated her needs. And that he'd wanted her and Megan to ride out the storm here at the ranch.

"You have no idea how terrified I was when that barn came down on you." His expression took on a more simmering mood. His eyes narrowed, his nostrils flared. "This stupid ranch is nothing but a source of trouble." His gaze bore into her. "I don't know what I'd do if I lost you again."

Carly froze.

Lost? To lose, one must have possession in the first place. Did he have her? Or her heart, anyway?

Uncomfortable with the intensity of his stare, she took a sip, peering out the picture window at a sea of white. "Looks like things are improving out there." The ferocious winds of last night had died down, though they still had the capability to send snow drifting across the open range, hindered only by the mountains that stood in the distance.

"Thankfully." His agitation seemingly waning, he retreated to the overstuffed sofa and motioned for her to join him. "Did you sleep okay?"

After an indecisive moment, she eased onto the comfy cushions. "Like a rock. How about you?"

"Ditto." He reached his arm around her then, as though it were the most natural thing in the world, caressing her no doubt reckless curls with his fingers. The gesture, as opposed to the cold this time, sent a wave of chill bumps skittering down her arm. "Because I knew you and Megan were safe."

Her heart raced with anticipation. A thousand what-ifs played across her mind. Were these the actions of an old flame turned friend? Or did Andrew truly feel something more for her?

Movement caught her eye before she could assess things further. Megan shuffled toward them in her fleece pajamas, her strawberry blond hair in full bed-head mode.

"Good morning, sunshine." Andrew inched over, allowing her to sit between them.

Her daughter gave a sleepy smile as she snuggled between them.

"Sleep well?" Carly laid her head against her daughter's.

These were the moments she cherished. The quiet times with just her and Megan.

Except it wasn't just them. Andrew was there, too. And in that moment, it was as if they were a family. Her, Megan and Andrew.

Her heart rate accelerated again. Did she dare to dream? Dare to consider a future that consisted of something besides just her and her daughter?

With Andrew it would be so easy.

But she wasn't cut out for marriage. Or rather, marriage wasn't cut out for her.

No, there would be no fairy-tale endings for her. She gave up on dreams when Dennis lost interest in her as his wife. He no longer wanted her. When he died, they were simply two people existing in the same house. Definitely not the kind of marriage she'd envisioned.

She wasn't about to travel down that road again. A road littered with broken promises and shattered dreams. Besides, Andrew was going back to Denver in a few weeks, anyway. So the sooner she got back to town, back to Livie's house, back into the B and B, and back to her old life, the better off she'd be.

The lights in the kitchen came on then. The timing couldn't have been better.

She pushed to her feet. "Breakfast will be ready soon." And, Lord willing, she and Megan would be on their way back to town shortly thereafter.

Thanks to a gas stove, they'd just finished a breakfast of pancakes and bacon when Jude called from town to let them know that the power was out all over Ouray proper. Information that suited Andrew just fine. Because the more reasons he had to keep Carly and Megan at the ranch, the better. And since his grandmother's house had neither a working fireplace nor a generator, there wasn't any room for Carly to argue.

While she gave his father a breathing treatment, Andrew took Megan to the stables to feed the foals. Now that the wind had died down, things weren't too bad outside.

"Whose snowmobile?" Megan pointed to the machine Noah had parked outside the stable. Evidently his brother had been too lazy to walk this morning.

"That would be Noah's."

"Oh." She frowned, adjusting her shimmery purple stocking cap.

"What's wrong?"

"I was just thinking how fun it would be for you, me and Mommy to go for a ride."

"I see." He couldn't say he blamed her. Being cooped up inside was never fun. Especially when you were a kid. And there were no other kids around.

He reached for the door to the stable. "You know, we have two more back at the house."

"Really?" She stepped inside, her entire face lighting up. "Could you take us for a ride? Oh, please, please, please." She clapped her purple mittens together.

The sight made him chuckle. Come to think of it, he hadn't been snowmobiling in forever. Odd, since it was something he'd always enjoyed.

Surrounded by the smell of hay and horses, he looked down at Megan. How could he turn down such a cute plea?

"It's okay with me. But it's almost lunchtime, so we'd better wait until after that. And only if your mama agrees."

"Yay!" She threw her fists into the air like Rocky Balboa and danced around.

"But first we need to feed Elsa and Anna."

While Megan gave the rapidly growing foals their bottles, he found Noah adding fresh hay to the stalls and put a bug in his ear about her request. He knew good and well that Carly wouldn't leave his father unless someone was there to look after him.

By the time they arrived back at the house, Carly was at the stove, working on grilled ham-and-cheese sandwiches and tomato soup.

In her eagerness, Megan practically stumbled right out of her boots trying to get to her. "Mommy, Andrew said he would take us for a snowmobile ride. Please, please, can we go?"

Carly flipped another sandwich. "We're about to have lunch."

"No, *after* lunch."

Turning ever so slightly, her mother narrowed her pretty blue eyes on him while addressing her daughter. "Sweetie, we'll need to go home soon."

He didn't get it. Carly had seemed fine when she woke up this morning. But ever since breakfast, she'd been more…standoffish. And he didn't have the slightest clue why.

"Not as long as the electricity is out." He grabbed a carrot stick from the bowl on the counter and bit off the end. "You two will freeze."

She pursed her lips, returning her attention to Megan. "Okay, you can go for a short ride after lunch."

"What about you?" Megan cocked her head, her bottom lip slightly pooched out. "I want you to go, too."

"I have to take care of Mr. Clint."

"I can do that." Noah's timing couldn't have been better. "You go on and have fun with Andrew and Megan."

Now that all of her objections had been overcome…

Andrew lifted a brow. "What do you say, Carly? You used to enjoy snowmobiling when we were kids."

She removed one sandwich and added more butter to the pan before answering. "I suppose a short ride wouldn't hurt."

He wasn't sure what she considered short, but he planned to make the best of it.

When lunch was over and the kitchen was clean, Andrew and Megan went outside while Carly settled Dad in for a nap. Andrew needed to make sure the largest of the machines, one all three of them could ride on, was gassed up and ready to go.

"This is going to be so much fun." Megan watched his every move.

He sure hoped so. The whole notion of a snowmobile ride didn't seem all that appealing to Carly. Something he found rather strange considering she used to plow circles around him when they were younger. A fact she never let him forget.

After returning the gas can to the shed beside the house, he fired up the machine. Revving the engine, he looked at Megan. "Shall we take 'er for a test run?"

No having to ask her twice. She hurried off of the deck and hopped on behind him.

He handed her a helmet. "Safety first."

She tugged it on, and he helped her fasten it before taking a spin around the house.

When they returned, Carly was waiting on the deck, helmet tucked under her arm as she pulled on her gloves. "Are you purposely trying to wake your father?"

He glanced back at Megan, who was wearing the same uh-oh expression he was. "Did we really wake him?"

"No. But with all that racket, you could have." She slipped her helmet on, then climbed aboard, wedging her daughter between her and Andrew. "Drive someplace *away* from the house, please."

He eased on the thumb throttle until they were a good ways from the house before picking up speed. Snow was flying as they bounded over the frozen pasture, headed toward the river. Behind him, Megan wasn't the only one laughing. Obviously Carly had changed her tune. Or rather, the ride had changed it.

When they reached the river, he killed the engine. They all climbed off the machine and removed their helmets.

"That was so much fun." Megan's smile was rivaled only by her mother's.

"Yeah, it was." He smoothed a hand over his hair, his gaze drifting to Carly. "It's been a long time since I've done that."

"Me, too." Leaving her helmet on the machine, Carly shoved her hands into the pockets of her puffy jacket. "I think the last time I did it was with you." She surveyed the river and the mountains just beyond. "And I believe we ended up right about here."

"Can I go exploring?" Megan squinted up at her mother.

"Yes. But stay away from the river."

"Okay." The kid took off down the bank, past the large cottonwood tree he and his brothers used to swing on.

He eyed Carly. "Shall we follow her?"

She smiled then. "Please."

As they walked, his mind flooded with memories. Most of which included Carly. "I guess we used to come down here a lot back in high school."

She watched her daughter scoop up a mound of snow, shape it into a ball and throw it at a tree. "We sure did. I've always loved it out here."

"Really? Why?"

She sent him a frustrated look. "Andrew, you have got to stop being so negative about this place and focus on all the good things the ranch has to offer." She swept an arm through the air. "Do you not see this? It's so peaceful here. It's easy to understand why your parents loved this ranch so much. They had their own little refuge from the world."

He glanced around. Too many struggles for him to see it that way.

He turned back to her. Through her eyes, though, everything looked better.

"I guess we did do a lot of walking along this path." Of course, it wasn't so much about where they were as it was just being with her. He focused on the river. "I was always comfortable sharing things with you. Like I could tell you anything and you'd understand."

Whap!

"Hey!" He twisted to see Megan grinning at him.

"Gotcha." She pointed to the spot where her snowball had struck him in the arm.

"Oh, so that's how you want to play." He scooped up a wad of snow and packed it into a ball before taking aim at Megan.

"Missed me—"

His second shot was a direct hit.

Next thing he knew, it was every man for himself. Except he was the only man, and Carly and Megan had joined forces against him.

As the snowballs continued to fly, he charged Carly, tackling her into a snowdrift.

Both winded, they stared at one another as their breaths hovered in the chilly air. Holding her in his arms, their faces so close…

"You know, we didn't always just talk while we were out here," he whispered.

For a moment, her eyes searched his, as though they were lost in time. Then the redness in her cheeks deepened. She rolled to her side, and he helped her to her feet.

"We'd better get back to the house," she said, dusting the snow from her pants. "I don't want to leave your father for too long."

Reluctantly he fired up the snowmobile. Him and his big mouth.

When they arrived at the house, his brother Jude was pulling up.

Still wearing his police uniform, he got out of his truck and met them on the deck. "Looks like you guys were out having some fun."

"It was awesome," said Megan.

Jude turned his attention to Carly. "You'll be glad to know that the electricity's back on in town."

"That's excellent news." Smiling, she glanced at her daughter first, then at Andrew. "I'll just check on your father and we'll be on our way."

So much for trying to keep her at the ranch. Now he needed to figure out why she was suddenly so eager to leave.

Chapter Thirteen

Carly was glad to be back home, or at least to Livie's house, instead of under the same roof as Andrew. But by noon Saturday, she couldn't help feeling that the ranch was where she needed to be. Though it had nothing to do with Andrew and everything to do with Clint.

Okay, perhaps a small part of it had to do with Andrew.

She transferred a batch of peanut butter cookies from baking sheet to cooling rack, the sweet aroma beckoning her to sample just one. Maybe two. Or ten.

Resisting, she set the empty baking pan aside and blew out an annoyed breath. In her eagerness to get away from Andrew and the crazy notions his presence seemed to evoke, she'd practically abandoned his father. Sure, Noah and Andrew knew how to give him breathing treatments and would see to it that he took his medicine, but would they monitor him as closely as she did? Would they remember to take his temperature? And what if Andrew needed to work on her kitchen to make up for the time lost to the storm? Without her there to look after Clint, he wouldn't be able to leave.

Megan shuffled into the kitchen from the parlor, eyeing the cookies. "Ooo, can I have one?"

"Help yourself." The more Megan ate, the fewer there were to tempt her.

Her daughter grabbed a treat before dropping into one of the faux leather swivel chairs at the table. She swung her leg back and forth. "I'm bored."

She wasn't the only one.

Grabbing a cookie for herself, Carly rounded the peninsula to join Megan at the table. "What would you like to do?"

Megan broke off a piece of cookie. "Can we go to the ranch? I'm worried about Elsa and Anna."

"You don't think Andrew and Noah can take care of them?"

"Yeah, but it's not the same."

Just like having the brothers care for Clint wasn't the same. "You're right. It's not."

She bit into her cookie, the peanutty taste sending her taste buds into a frenzy. Hard to believe it hadn't even been a week since Clint's pneumonia was diagnosed. Meaning he was far from being out of the woods.

You said you would take care of him.

And even argued against them bringing in someone else to do so. Yet she'd bailed, all because things got a little too cozy with Andrew. If that didn't sound like a coward, Carly wasn't sure what did.

She polished off her cookie and stood, dusting the crumbs from her hands. "Okay, let's go."

Under a crisp blue sky, they headed north on Main Street in her SUV. Seemed the warmer temperatures had brought out all of Ouray today. The sidewalks were bustling with people. With the storm past, everyone was eager to be out and about and, no doubt, ready for spring. Herself included.

Continuing outside of town, Carly found herself second-guessing her impromptu decision. Maybe she should have called first. After all, she'd left them high and dry. What if the Stephens men were upset with her?

Butterflies took wing in her midsection as she pulled into the ranch. This was such a bad idea.

No, leaving so abruptly yesterday was.

Bumping up the long drive, she tightened her grip on the steering wheel. Too late to turn back now.

They had barely come to a stop when Megan grabbed the container of cookies Carly had made, hopped out of the vehicle and started up the deck. Oh, no. Megan was used to following Andrew into the house. What if she walked in without knocking?

Carly shoved her door open and planted her booted feet on the wet gravel. "Megan!"

Her daughter stopped immediately. Looked at her.

She sucked in a calming breath. "Wait for me, please."

A few moments later, the two of them knocked.

When Andrew swung the door open, his expression was somewhere between surprise and relief. Though his smile told her he was glad to see them.

"How's Clint?" She stepped into the mudroom, breathing a little easier.

"Not too good, I'm afraid."

Her breathing all but stopped. This was her fault. If she hadn't run out on them...

"He's refusing his breathing treatments." Exasperation creased Andrew's forehead. "Won't even let me take his temperature."

"That's not good." And the fact that she could hear the older man wheezing before she was halfway to the family room escalated her concern.

Pushing up the sleeves of her light blue Henley, she knelt beside Clint's recliner. "What's this I hear about you not taking your breathing treatments?" She hated the annoyance in her voice, especially since it was directed more at her than him.

He looked at her with a mischievous grin. "I was just thinking I might oughta do one."

Okay, now she was annoyed with him. Had he been refusing them on purpose?

She pushed to her feet, dug her fists into her hips. "Clint, do you want to get well or not?"

He brought his chair to an upright position. "Now, don't go gettin' yourself all worked up. I said I'd do one."

"Mmm-hmm. And what if I hadn't shown up?"

Despite looking somewhat pale, there was a glint in his eye as he glared at her. "Guess we'll never know."

Guilt kept her quiet and had her stepping aside to ready the nebulizer.

"You need to take your medicine, Mr. Clint, so you can come to the stables and see Elsa and Anna." Her daughter looked very serious as she addressed the older man. "They're getting bigger every day."

"That's 'cause they've got you takin' care of them," he said.

"Speaking of Elsa and Anna—" Andrew smiled down at Megan "—would you like to go see them?"

"Uh-huh." Her head bobbed like crazy with excitement. Then again, those horses were her main reason for wanting to come out here.

"Where's Noah?" Deciding she'd better take Clint's temp before the breathing treatment, Carly retrieved the thermometer from the side table.

"Checking horses and cattle." Andrew was already on his way into the mudroom with a happy Megan. Carly genuinely appreciated his attentiveness to her daughter. Something Megan had rarely received from her father.

Alone with Clint, Carly pulled the beeping thermometer from his mouth. 98.8. Not too bad. "You were being stubborn again, weren't you?"

"I love my sons dearly, but they don't have your bedside manner."

His words pricked her heart. He wasn't just counting on her. He trusted her.

She shoved the thermometer back into its case, finding it tough to look him in the eye. "I'm sorry for deserting you."

Grabbing the nebulizer mask, she tugged on the elastic band.

Before she could slip it over his head, he reached a hand up to stop her. "Carly, I'd like to ask you a favor."

Lowering her hands, she said, "What's that?"

"I'd like you to help me keep Andrew in Ouray."

Confusion narrowed her gaze. "Keep him in Ouray? For how long?"

"Forever."

Her heart tripped and stuttered. Andrew in Ouray? Forever? What would that mean for her? For them? Staying away from him was challenging enough as it was.

"But Andrew's built a life in Denver," she said. "He's about to close on a new business. Besides, you give me too much credit. What could I possibly do to make Andrew want to stay in Ouray?"

"All Denver has done is steal his joy. When he first got here, his eyes had lost their spark. But now…he looks better than ever. And you're partly to thank for that." He wagged a finger in her direction. "You, my dear, have far more influence over my son than you think."

Carly begged to differ. If anyone had influence, it was Andrew. Every time she saw him, she felt like a teenager again. He was her first kiss. Her first love.

But he'd chosen work over her. Just like Dennis had done.

"Mind if I think on it for a bit?"

Lips pursed, he sent her a frustrated look. "Don't take too long. We haven't got much time."

Standing again, she slipped the mask over Clint's face. For his sake, she might drop a few hints to Andrew if the opportunity presented itself. For her heart's sake, though, she couldn't help hoping they'd fall on a deaf ear. If Andrew stayed, he'd fight even harder to keep his grandmother's house. Leaving her dreams of expanding the B and B in the dust.

By Tuesday, Dad was doing noticeably better. His color was back, there hadn't been any fever spikes since the weekend, and the coughing and wheezing had subsided considerably. All because of Carly and the care she'd been giving him.

Andrew was envious. He wished he could spend as much time with her as his father had. Because if there was one thing he'd learned since returning to Ouray, it was that life was better with Carly around.

Lately, though, they barely crossed paths. Only when he brought Megan to the ranch after school. Even then, Carly didn't seem to have time to stop and talk like before. Instead, she'd get dinner on the table and she and Megan would be on their way.

Sometimes he couldn't help wondering if she was purposely avoiding him. Ever since the blizzard, things had been different, though he didn't have a clue why.

He wound his truck past the red sandstone formations north of Ouray. In the last few days he'd made great strides in bringing Carly's old home back to life. The mitigation team had completed their work over the weekend, allowing him to get started on the floors.

He frowned. Now that the refinishing process was complete, he'd need to allow a couple of days for the floors to dry. This would be the perfect time for him to get some work done on his grandmother's house. But with Carly and Megan living there, that was out of the question.

Hands on the steering wheel, he eyed the open rangeland with its rapidly dwindling snowpack. He and Carly hadn't even discussed Grandma's place since the fire. But now that things were winding down at Granger House, leaving him only a couple of weeks before the closing on Magnum Homes, he'd need to find a way to bring it up. As a businessman, he could appreciate Carly wanting to expand the B and B. But as the great-grandson of the man who built the house in question, he refused to let it leave the family. Something Carly should understand better than anyone.

Turning in to the ranch with Megan, he hoped that maybe tonight he could convince Carly to stay for dinner. Or that he could at least carve out a little time to talk with her before she left.

"Are you looking forward to seeing your grandparents?" Carly's in-laws had invited Megan to come and visit during spring break next week.

"Uh-huh." She craned her neck, trying to see the corral as they continued past the stable. No doubt looking for the foals. "My cousin, Mia, is going to be there. We always have fun. Who's here?" She pointed to the unfamiliar white SUV parked beside his father's dually.

"I don't know," he said.

He eased the pickup to a stop, surveying the dingy ranch house in front of him and the partially collapsed barn in his rearview mirror. There never had been any shortage of work around this place, but he'd never seen things look this bad, either. He supposed he could help. If he had the time. Which he didn't. At least, not now.

Grabbing his thermos, he exited the truck. He could hardly wait to see what kind of food Carly had waiting for them today. He really did enjoy walking into the house and being greeted with the aromas of fresh baked sweets and dinner in progress.

When he and Megan entered the mudroom, they were met with the sound of laughter. And a voice he didn't recognize.

He sniffed the air. Carly had been baking, all right, but where was the savory smell of tonight's meal?

Disappointment wove through him, even though he knew it was wrong. It wasn't like Carly was their maid. She was taking care of his father out of the goodness of her heart, and he had no right to expect anything more. Yet he did want more. He liked coming home to her. Liked sharing the events of his day with her.

He supposed he'd better get used to it, though. Because once he went back to Denver, he'd have no one.

Inside the family room, Dad sat upright in his recliner, while Carly was on the couch beside the blond-haired woman who'd stopped by Granger House right after the fire. What was her name? Hillary something.

Dad was the first to see them. "There they are." He held his arms out. "How's my favorite nine-year-old?"

Megan giggled, dropped her backpack and gave the old man a hug.

"How was school?" Dad had become quite enamored with Megan over the past week or so. The kid had a way of bringing out the best in his old man.

"I got a hundred on my math test."

"Excellent."

"News like that deserves a brownie." Carly stood, eyeing Megan first, then Andrew, before continuing into the kitchen. "You remember Ms. Hillary, don't you?"

Megan waved. "Hi." Seemingly shy, she remained beside his father.

"Good to see you again, Hillary." Andrew nodded in her direction.

The woman studied him a moment. "Yes. We met the day of the fire, correct?"

"Yes, ma'am."

"Hillary and I were in school together," said Dad.

"Though I was much younger than your father," she was quick to add.

"Three years isn't that much difference." The old man frowned.

Carly returned with a plate of brownies in one hand and a stack of napkins in the other. She offered a treat to Megan first, along with a napkin, then continued around the room. "Hillary brought dinner for you guys."

You guys? As in just him, Dad and Noah?

"Pot roast, smashed potatoes…" Hillary waved a hand. "Celeste does so much cooking anyway, we're never going to know when that nesting urge hits her."

Carly set the plate on the side table at the end of the couch. "If she's anything like me, she'll be cleaning everything in sight a couple days before going into labor."

Hillary touched a long fingernail to her lips. "Yes, I seem to recall that when I was close to delivering Celeste, too."

"Hillary Ward. A grandmother." His father's smile held a definite air of mischief. "I always thought world domination woulda been more your style."

"That's Hillary Ward-Thompson." The woman pushed to her feet. "And no, darling, not *world*. I prefer corporate domination."

"So how come you're back in Ouray?" Dad looked up at her, one graying brow lifted in amusement.

She tugged on the hem of her crisp white blouse. "According to my doctor, I put too much of my heart into my job and it couldn't keep up. So, considering I have two granddaughters now and another grandchild on the way, I decided there were better ways to spend my time than jet-setting across the globe."

"Woman, you're too young to retire."

"Who said anything about retiring?" Hillary glared at his father. "I'm merely redirecting my focus."

Andrew caught Carly smiling at the pair. Not that he could blame her. Watching the interaction between Hillary and his father was more entertaining than most television shows.

His phone rang in his pocket. He pulled it out to see his attorney's name on the screen. "Excuse me, please." He made his way down the hall to his bedroom. "What's up, Ned?"

"Hey, good news. I just got word that the closing date for Magnum has been moved up."

"Moved up?" A few weeks ago, that would have been great news. But now… "To when?"

"Two weeks from today."

"Two weeks?" He raked a hand through his hair. Granger House would barely be done by then. What about his grandmother's house? That had been his sole purpose in coming back to Ouray in the first place.

"I think the sister is afraid her brother will change his mind."

Change his mind? But they had an agreement.

"That time frame isn't going to be a problem, is it?"

He stared out the window, eyeing the mountains just past the river. "Sorry. My father's been ill. And I've been busy with a project." Not the one he'd initially intended, but one he was coming to wish would never end. "I'll be there, though. Go ahead and email me the details."

A lead weight formed in his stomach as he ended the call. Why did they have to move the closing up? Usually it was the other way around. And for once, he would have preferred it that way. Because for the first time in his life, he actually wanted to be in Ouray.

Chapter Fourteen

Carly wanted to keep her baby here at home.

Watching Megan pack, she tried to douse the ache in her heart with another cup of tea, all the while keeping one eye glued to the window, waiting for the Wagners' arrival. Sure, Megan had gone to visit Dennis's parents before, but never without her. Like it or not, though, her daughter was growing up. And it was important that she maintain a relationship with her father's parents.

Still, the kid didn't have to act so excited about leaving.

If only Carly could go with her. But between the repairs at Granger House, helping with the foals and looking in on Clint, there was no way she could break away.

She huffed out a breath. Sometimes being a grown-up was such a pain. She'd much rather throw herself on the floor and kick and scream until Megan agreed to stay.

"There they are!" Megan practically squealed. She rushed to the bed and tugged her new Hello Kitty suitcase onto the floor. The *thwamp, thwamp, thwamp* of the wheels as she rolled it across the wooden planks was like a hammer to Carly's heart.

Willing herself to remain calm, she joined her daughter in the parlor as Megan threw open the door.

"Mia's here, too." Both Megan's fists went into the air and she jumped in circles. "Yay!"

Carly peered out the window with the sudden suspicion that having Megan visit was more Mia's idea than her grandparents'. She didn't doubt that the Wagners loved her daughter, but she often got the feeling that Megan was more of an afterthought because she didn't live in Grand Junction like their other grandchildren. Something they'd tried to change for years when Dennis was alive. His parents had played a big role in Dennis's push to move there.

Shaking away the less than pleasant thoughts, Carly set her mug on a coaster atop a side table and moved on to the door.

Mia had rushed ahead of her grandparents, and she and Megan were already hugging on the porch.

Carly pushed the storm door open.

Beverly Wagner waved and gave a half smile as she meandered up the walk. Of course, she never actually looked at Carly. She was too busy scrutinizing Livie's house. Granted, it hadn't been modernized and wasn't in pristine condition, but it was still charming and comfortable. Not to mention convenient. And far better than a hotel room.

Behind Beverly, her husband, Chuck, made eye contact and grinned. "Hello, Carly." He always was the more laid back of the two, able to see the good in everything. Including her.

After a round of hugs and a report on details of the fire, Carly took them next door to Granger House to show them the progress on her new kitchen.

Passing through the front door, she said, "I'm still amazed that they managed to get rid of the smoke smell."

Megan pinched her nose. "It was *disgusting.*"

Chuck smiled and ruffled his granddaughter's hair.

"From what I hear, those restoration teams are pretty good."

"And here's your proof." Carly gestured to the sitting area in the parlor. "Not a trace of soot or smoke." Everything there looked virtually the same way it had before. She drew in a relieved breath. "We were blessed that the fire was contained to the kitchen and family room."

"Yes, you were." Chuck came alongside her, wrapping an arm around her shoulders. "And we're thankful that neither you nor Megan was hurt."

Beverly hugged Megan, a genuine smile lighting her typically sober face. "Yes, we are."

Tears pricked the backs of Carly's eyes. Blinking, she led them into the dining room where, again, everything had been restored. The ceiling and walls were soot-free and the antique furniture cleaned. Even the molding around the door, the one that had been charred, looked the way it used to. "I still can't believe this room was untouched by either the fire or the water."

At the opening to the kitchen, she paused. "But this is where we took the worst hit." Excitement bubbled inside as she tugged the protective plastic sheeting to one side, allowing Mia and the Wagners to see in.

"They just installed the cabinets yesterday." She led them into the space. In addition to the cabinets, the freshly painted drywall made everything look so fresh and new, despite the wires that still peeked out of holes where light fixtures, switches and outlets would go. "Andrew covered the floors with this paper so they wouldn't get scratched. But they're a beautiful dark walnut color. Andrew said—"

"Who's Andrew?" Beverly's judgmental gaze narrowed and shifted to Carly.

"My contractor."

"Her *boy*friend." Megan giggled with her cousin, grinning like a goofball, batting her eyelashes.

Perhaps telling her goodbye might be easier than she first thought. "Megan… Andrew and I are friends, but he is *not* my boyfriend."

Megan fisted her hands on her hips, drew her eyebrows downward. "Well, he should be." She looked up at her grandparents. "He's really nice. And he has a ranch."

Carly cringed. While she appreciated Megan's fondness for Andrew, this kind of talk was putting her in a very awkward position.

She turned to her in-laws and forced a smile. "His father has a ranch. Andrew lives in Denver. He's visiting his father." She then glared at Megan, albeit ever so subtly.

Though Beverly didn't say anything, Carly couldn't help noticing the look of disapproval on her face. The silent commentary the woman no doubt had regarding Carly being seen with another man.

By the time they pulled away ten minutes later, Carly wasn't sure if she wanted to cheer or cry. In the end, crying won out. Four whole days without her baby. How would she survive?

The best thing she could do now was redirect her attention. Find something else to concentrate on besides her daughter's absence.

Considering she'd focused on few things besides her daughter in the last nine years, that was going to be tough. The only person she could think of who needed her attention now was Clint. And even he didn't really need her anymore. Still, she'd agreed to take care of him and that's just what she'd do.

And in the evenings, after tending to what little bookkeeping she had, she might even make some headway on

Mona's scrapbooks. With Clint's approval, she'd brought all of the boxes back to Livie's earlier this week.

She gathered her things to head to the ranch, yet before she could make it out the door, another round of tears had her reaching for a box of tissues. The doorbell interrupted her pity party, though.

Dabbing her eyes, she drew in two deep breaths and opened the door to find Andrew standing on her front porch.

He opened the storm door. "You miss her already, don't you?"

All she could do was nod as tears streamed down her cheeks once again. Talk about a poor excuse for a grown-up.

Moving inside, Andrew enveloped her in his strong embrace. The smell of fresh air and coffee wrapped around her as he stroked her back, her hair.

She savored his strength. And boy, did he feel good.

"How about this?" He set her away from him.

Still lost in the fog of his embrace, she struggled to focus.

"Tell me one thing that you've been dying to do but couldn't do with Megan."

She hadn't done anything without considering Megan in…ever. She shrugged, forcing her brain to think. "I don't know. Go see a movie at the theater." She looked up at Andrew. "One of *my* choosing."

He stood there staring at her as though she'd lost her mind. Then… "Get your jacket. We're going to the movies."

Carly watched him, recalling the look in her mother-in-law's eye when they discussed Andrew. Going to the movies with him would be almost like a…a date.

And what would be wrong with that?

Clint. "Wait, wait, wait… What about your father? What if he needs help?"

"Sorry, I forgot to tell you. Daniel's back home."

"When did he get in?"

"Last night. Noah and I have filled him in on everything, and since he's eager to spend some time with the old man…" He held out his hand. "This day is all about you."

Andrew couldn't bear to see Carly so sad. When he arrived at his grandmother's house early this afternoon, his intention had been to discuss their joint ownership and what to do with the place. But after seeing the heartwrenching look on her face, he couldn't bear to broach the topic. All he wanted now was to see Carly smile.

"So, what would you like to see?" Standing in front of the movie theater in Montrose, the bright midday sun shining down on them, he watched Carly as she stared at the marquee. Considering there were only three shows to choose from, it shouldn't take her long to decide. Not like the multiplexes in Denver that showed twenty-plus movies all at the same time.

"Well, they are showing that new romantic comedy with Matthew McConaughey. But I hate to do that to you."

"Do what to me?"

"Make you sit through a rom-com."

"Are you kidding?" He stepped in front of her now. "I happen to be a big Matthew McConaughey fan." Though he would have preferred a nice horror flick. Something good and scary that would have Carly reaching for him.

"No, you're not."

He slapped a hand to his chest and stumbled backward. "Madam, it wounds me that you would question my sincerity."

She looked at him with pretty, tear-free blue eyes. "Okay, fine. Mr. McConaughey it is, then."

They purchased their tickets then headed straight for the snack bar. After all, neither of them had eaten lunch, and the aroma of popcorn was too powerful to resist.

"Would you like butter on that?" The freckle-faced girl on the other side of the counter eyed him first, then Carly.

"Definitely," said Carly. "Oh, and a box of Junior Mints, too, please."

Andrew wrinkled his nose. "You still dump those things in the popcorn like you used to?"

"Of course. How else are you going to get that whole sweet and salty experience?"

Andrew caught the girl's attention. "Make that two popcorns, please."

Carly elbowed him in the ribs. "You didn't used to complain."

"Because back then I had enough money for only one popcorn." Grinning, he reached for his wallet. "Now I can afford my own."

The sun had drifted into the western sky when they left the theater a couple of hours later.

"Okay, I'll admit it," he said as they strolled across the parking lot. "That was a pretty good movie."

"What do you mean, admit? I thought you were a big McConaughey fan?"

He stopped beside the truck. "I am. But not *every* movie can be great."

She laughed, shaking her head. "You're such a goof."

"Perhaps." Leaning toward her, he rested one hand against the truck, effectively trapping her. "But am I a cute goof?"

Her gaze lifted to his. "Maybe."

His eyes drifted to her lips, lingering there for one

excruciating moment as he contemplated kissing her. "What's something else having Megan around stops you from doing?"

After a moment, her smile turned mischievous. "Eating dessert first."

While it wasn't exactly the answer he was hoping for, he couldn't help laughing. He straightened and opened her door. "What have you got in mind? Ice cream, cake, pie…? Or maybe something more decadent like a crème brûlée?"

She let go a soft gasp. "I *love* crème brûlée."

That dreamy look on her face was all the encouragement he needed. "One crème brûlée coming up."

He drove them to one of Montrose's finer dining establishments.

"Andrew, I'm not dressed for a place like this."

He looked at her skinny jeans, riding-style boots and long gray shirt. "What are you talking about? You look great."

Since it was still early, they were seated right away, and in a cozy booth, no less. Something that wouldn't have happened in another hour or two. Not on a Saturday evening.

He promptly ordered two crème brûlées, then leaned back against the tufted leather cushion.

"Thank you." Across the table, Carly rested her chin on her hand and stared at him. "I wasn't sure I was going to make it through this day and—" she smiled "—you've turned it into something wonderful."

"You deserve it." He sent her a wink.

Blushing, she unfolded her white linen napkin and placed it in her lap, all the while taking in the river rock fireplace and the rustic wood beams. "So, tell me about your life in Denver. I haven't heard you talk about it much."

"Probably because there's not much to talk about."

Her gaze jerked to his so fast he was surprised she didn't get whiplash. "Oh, come on, Andrew. You owned one of the most successful commercial construction companies in Denver. I'm sure your life is anything but boring."

He lifted a brow. "How do you know Pinnacle Construction was successful?"

"Because your father told me."

"Oh." A minor ding to his pride. He was kind of hoping she'd Googled him or something. Not that there'd be much to find.

The waitress approached. "Two crème brûlées." She set Carly's in front of her before serving his. "Can I get you anything else?"

"Not right now," he said.

Carly was the first to crack through the caramelized sugar, coming up with a spoonful of custard.

"Cheers." She lifted her spoon into the air, then shoved it into her mouth. Her eyes closed as she savored the dessert.

"Any good?"

"Best I've ever tasted."

"Good." He cracked the hardened shell on his brûlée, knowing he needed to answer her question, to tell her something about himself. But what? "Life in Denver isn't much different than living anywhere else. There's work, church…" He took a bite. "Mmm…"

"What do you do when you're not at work?" Watching him, she scooped another spoonful.

Unfortunately, there wasn't much to his life outside work. He'd rather stay at the office than go home to an empty house. Not that he'd tell her that. "The usual stuff. Watch TV, go to the gym." Man, did he lead a pathetic life or what?

At least here he had his dad or one of his brothers to keep him company. He glanced across the table. Though, given the choice, he'd rather spend his time with Carly and Megan. With them, even normal, everyday stuff was more fun.

He managed to change the subject by bringing up an old classmate, and by the time they finished their dessert, he'd caught up on just about everyone in Ouray, both old and new. And as the lights dimmed, he asked the waitress to bring menus again so they could order dinner.

After their food arrived, he knew it was time for him to share one more thing with her. He could only pray it wouldn't ruin the whole night.

"My lawyer called this week." He cut into his prime rib. "Seems they've moved up the closing date on my new business."

"I guess you're looking forward to it, huh?" Was it his imagination or was there a hint of disappointment in her tone? "Home builder, right?"

"Yes. Custom homes." He stabbed another piece of meat. "I learned about it just before I closed on my old company. The owner passed away unexpectedly and neither of his kids was interested in the business. Seemed like the perfect opportunity." Of course, that was before he came to Ouray. "Don't worry, though. I'll have your kitchen completed and you'll be moved back into Granger House before I leave."

To his relief, she smiled. "I know you will."

"I just hope Dad's back on his feet by then."

"You worry about him, don't you?" She cocked her head, poking at her seafood pasta with her fork.

"It's no secret that I was so wrapped up in my work, I didn't make it back home before my mother died. I don't want to make that mistake again."

Reaching across the table, she laid her hand atop his. "Your mother knew that you loved her, Andrew."

"I know. But I never got to say goodbye. And that will always haunt me." He wanted to kick himself as soon as the words left his mouth. *You're trying to make her smile, not depress her.*

Fortunately, the conversation was on the upswing by the time the waitress delivered their check. It was well after dark when they arrived back in Ouray. He walked Carly to the door of his grandmother's house and escorted her inside.

"Thank you for a wonderful time." Her smile, different from any he'd seen all day, and exactly what he'd set out to achieve, did strange things to his insides. "I can't remember the last time I had so much fun."

"Like I said earlier, you deserve it." Unable to stop himself, he caressed her cheek. "You give so much of yourself to others. But surely we didn't cover everything. So if there's something else you'd like to do before Megan comes home—"

"As a matter of fact, there is." She chewed her bottom lip.

"And what might that be?"

"This." Before he realized what was happening, she pushed up on her toes and kissed him. A kiss that nearly knocked him off his feet.

She started to pull away, but he wrapped his arms around her waist and pulled her closer. Her fingers threaded through the back of his hair as their lips met again. He could stay this way forever.

Because, whether he planned to or not, he had fallen in love with Carly all over again.

Chapter Fifteen

It had been a long time since someone had made Carly feel as special as Andrew had yesterday. He'd catered to her every whim and, at the same time, made her feel like a woman instead of just a mom, caretaker or friend. He'd awakened something in her she'd thought she'd never feel again. Something she was too afraid to name. Because acknowledging it left her open for disappointment. Heartbreak. And yet she'd kissed him.

What *had* she been thinking?

Now here she sat, wedged in a church pew between Andrew and Clint. Every time Andrew shifted the slightest bit, she caught a whiff of fresh air and masculinity that reminded her of that kiss.

As if she needed any reminder. She'd had a hard time thinking about anything else since it happened. Even now, her heart thundered at the memory. Here in church, of all places.

Straightening, she eyed the wooden cross over the pulpit, trying hard to focus on Pastor Dan's sermon. A message based on Isaiah 43. She smoothed a hand over the pages of her open Bible.

"Sometimes we get so bogged down in the past that

we forget to open our eyes to the future God has for us," the pastor said.

The future? Something she found very frightening. While her past might not be all that pretty, the future was unknown, and uncertainty was always scary. Especially when it involved the heart. Her gaze momentarily darted to Andrew.

If the future was so frightening, why did she keep thinking about that kiss and contemplating all sorts of what-ifs? Hadn't Andrew told her that he would be going back to Denver once her kitchen was done? That he was about to sign off on another business?

God, I know that anything You have for me is better than I could possibly want for myself. Help me not cling to what I want and be open to Your will.

In the meantime, she would immerse herself in Mona's scrapbooks and do whatever it took to stay away from Andrew.

After the service, the Stephens men congregated on the sidewalk outside the church, beside the towering white fir. Everyone except Matt, that is, who was on call with the sheriff's department.

While Carly wanted simply to whisk right past them, it would be rude for her not to say hello to Daniel, the youngest of the Stephens boys. This was the first she'd seen him since he'd returned from his latest adventure.

She eased beside him. "How was Peru?"

"Awesome." With his medium-length blond hair, blue eyes and sparkling smile, he looked like a young Brad Pitt. "Rafting the Cotahuasi River never gets old. You should try it sometime."

She practically burst out laughing. "Daniel, I haven't even rafted the Uncompahgre since I was a teenager. And that's in my own backyard."

He chuckled. "Why don't you join us for lunch and I'll show you some photos?"

Lunch? No. She had scrapbooks waiting for her. "I'm sorry. I can't—"

"'Course she's joining us." Clint rolled up the sleeves of his blue plaid button-down shirt.

Her gaze narrowed. "I'm surprised you're even here. You know, you still haven't been cleared by the doctor." Though, looking at him now, one would have a hard time believing he'd been sick. His color was back to normal, he was clean-shaven and, with his salt-and-pepper hair neatly combed, he looked quite handsome.

Lord willing, the doctor would give him the all-clear at his checkup tomorrow. The poor man had given up just about everything he loved to do these past couple of weeks, so she hoped he'd be allowed to return to most, if not all, of his normal activities around the ranch.

"It's only church. It's not like I'm out herdin' cattle." One corner of his mouth lifted then. "But if you're that worried, you'd best come on to the house and help these boys keep an eye on me."

She shook her head. "Don't think I don't know what you're up to, Clint." And even though she really would have loved to join them, the thought of spending another day with Andrew was what worried her most.

"You don't even have to cook," added Noah.

"That's right." The gleam in Andrew's brown eyes sent goose bumps down her spine. "We've got everything taken care of."

"Come on, Carly." Daniel nudged her with his elbow. "It'll be fun."

That's what she was afraid of.

She studied the conifers scattered around the vacant lot across the road, backdropped by Hayden Mountain. Perhaps it wouldn't hurt to go for a little bit. She could look at Daniel's pictures, have some lunch, then tell them she had a prior commitment and needed to leave. They didn't have to know it was the scrapbooks.

"You guys sure drive a hard bargain."

After a quick stop by Livie's to change clothes, she drove to the ranch. She could do this. Having everyone around would naturally deflect her attention away from Andrew.

When she entered the ranch house, her stomach growled at the mixture of smells. She was delighted to learn that they'd prepared elk burgers, homemade french fries, coleslaw and brownies. And they wouldn't let her set foot in the kitchen except to eat. These guys really did have a way of making a woman feel like a queen. Mona would have been proud.

After the meal, while Jude and Andrew cleaned up the kitchen and Clint settled in his recliner, Carly sat at the table with Daniel, poring over the photos on his tablet.

"That looks pretty intense," she said as he turned off the device.

"Most extreme white water in Peru."

"And you think I should try it?" She bumped him with her shoulder. "I think you need your head examined." Laughing, she looked up and saw Andrew leaning against the counter. Evidently they were done with the kitchen.

"Well, guys, I hate to cut this short." She stood and stretched. "But I have some things I need to take care of in town."

Each of them gave her a quick hug, except Andrew, who insisted on walking her out.

"I didn't know you needed to leave so soon," he said as they emerged onto the deck. "I was hoping we could go for a walk."

"I really—"

"Just a short one." His crooked smile made him look like the Andrew she remembered from high school. The one who had been able to talk her into just about anything.

Say no. No, no, no... "Okay."

He started toward the pasture. "Can you believe we're closing in on your completed kitchen?"

"Finally." She tilted her face heavenward, allowing the sun to warm her face. "It feels like it's taking *forever*." Though it also left her with a lot of mixed emotions. Once her kitchen was done, Andrew would be gone.

"You know what the preacher said this morning about not dwelling on the past?" Andrew took hold of her hand.

"Yes." Ignoring that annoying voice in her head, she entwined her fingers with his.

"Do you ever do that? Dwell on the past."

"More often than I care to admit."

"Me, too." He continued across the winter-weary landscape, looking straight ahead. "But then the verse he referenced went on to say that God was doing something new. And that 'Do you not perceive it?' part almost felt a smack upside my head. Like, 'Don't you get it, buddy? I'm working here.'"

She puffed out a laugh, eyeing the cattle in the distance.

"I'm not sure, Carly, but I think God is doing something new in my life."

"Like what?" She peered up at him, squinting against the sun's glare.

"I don't know." He drew to a stop beside the river, taking in the rushing water before looking at her. "Maybe it's this new business venture. But selling my company—something I never imagined I would do—coming back here and reconnecting with my family." He squeezed her hand and smiled. "Reconnecting with you."

Her heart pounded.

"And this ranch." He let go of her hand and bent to pick up a small rock. "Remember after the blizzard, when we came out here on the snowmobile?"

"Yes."

Tossing the pebble in his hand, he said, "You challenged me to start looking at the good things the ranch had to offer."

"I remember that." She picked up her own stone, rubbed its smooth surface with her thumb. "Though I think it was more of an order than a challenge."

He chuckled, throwing his rock into the water. "In that case, you'll be happy to know that I followed your orders." Hands slung low on his hips, he moved toward her. "Funny thing happened."

"What's that?"

"I'm actually enjoying the ranch, perhaps for the first time in my life."

She couldn't help but grin.

"Being here and talking with my brothers has brought back a lot of memories that have helped me realize that the hardships we endured while I was growing up were what bonded us together as a family and made us stronger. Not the other way around." He moved a step closer. "I know the ranch had nothing to do with my mother's death." He shrugged. "I was just looking for a scapegoat instead of taking responsibility for my actions."

Amid the soothing backdrop of the water, Carly's heart swelled. She'd been praying that God would help Andrew realize the truth. Now she could only pray that he would decide to stay in Ouray. Because despite trying to convince herself otherwise, she wanted him in her life.

* * *

Andrew drilled another screw into the hinge leaf for Carly's new pantry door, amazed at how quickly things had progressed.

It was only Tuesday, yet Dad was celebrating a clean bill of health by reclaiming his freedom as a rancher, and Carly's kitchen was nearing completion. Andrew wasn't sure how he felt about either one. Dad couldn't just pick up where he left off. He'd need to ease back into things after being laid up for two weeks. And as for Carly, Andrew would be fine with her project going into perpetuity.

Unfortunately, it didn't look like that was going to happen. The appliances had been delivered and installed yesterday, and thanks to Marianne's help and persistence in following up with their order, the marble countertops were set to be installed tomorrow. All he had left to do then was install the subway tile backsplash and hang the pendant lights over the island. Carly should be able to move back in before the weekend.

And he'd be on his way to Denver.

The thought making his heart ache, he leaned back against the doorjamb. He was in love with Carly again. Perhaps he'd never stopped. All these years and he'd never forgotten her. She was the standard by which all other women were judged. Not that he ever dated that much. Finding someone who even remotely understood him the way Carly did was next to impossible.

But he'd made a commitment to purchase Magnum Homes. Signed a contract. And he was nothing if not a man of his word.

He glanced around the space, pleased with how everything had come together. He and Carly made a good team. Now if they could just figure out what to do about his grandmother's house. Neither had broached the topic in weeks, and he was still clueless about how they were going to find a compromise.

He slid the screwdriver into his tool belt, grinning. He supposed he could marry her. That would keep the house in the family.

Yeah, right. If there's one thing he knew for sure, it was that Carly would never leave Ouray.

Still, if they couldn't come to some sort of agreement on what to do with Grandma's house, owning just half of it did neither one of them any good.

Movement outside the window on the opposite end of the kitchen drew his attention. Carly was just crossing the drive, bringing him lunch. Now that his father had been cleared, there was no reason for her to hang out at the ranch all day. Perhaps this would give them an opportunity to discuss his grandmother's house.

He hurried across the paper-covered floors to meet her at the door. At this point, he no longer wanted her to see the space until it was complete. Which reminded him, he needed to put paper over the windows, too, so she couldn't peek inside.

He swung open the door, quickly closing it behind him. "Why didn't you just text me? I could have come next door."

She sent him a shy smile. "Well, I was hoping to get a peek at any progress."

"Sorry." Hands on his hips, he blocked the door. "No more peeking until it's finished."

"But—"

He descended a couple of steps, then sat down. "Nice weather we're having today." Grinning, he perused the cloudless sky. "Good day for a picnic, don't you think?" He glanced back at her now. "And since you happen to be carrying a picnic basket…"

She sent him a pleading look. "Not even a little peek?"

"Nope."

Squaring her shoulders, she narrowed her gaze. "What if I said I'd withhold your lunch?"

He shrugged. "I have protein bars." Though they held about as much appeal as a brick compared to one of Carly's homemade meals. Still, he wasn't about to give in on this one.

"Okay, fine." She set the basket on the step in front of him with a thud.

"Hey—" leaning forward, he touched her cheek "—just think how exciting it will be to see everything done."

"I know." She lifted the basket lid. "But patience isn't my virtue." Reaching inside, she pulled out a foil-covered plate and handed it to him. "Hope you don't mind leftover fried chicken."

"Are you kidding?" He lifted the foil off the warm plate to discover mashed potatoes, corn and green beans, too. "There's no such thing as bad fried chicken."

She pulled out a plate for herself. "I was craving it last night, and since I'm alone, there's no way I could eat it all."

"And I get to reap the benefits." He bit into a drumstick. "This is delicious." He took hold of the napkin she offered and wiped his chin. "Seriously, you know you're spoiling me, don't you? I don't know what we're going to do at the ranch now that you're not there helping Dad."

"What can I say? I like to cook and take care of people."

"Well, your husband was a blessed man."

Carly's smile all but evaporated, and her pretty blue eyes clouded over. She set her plate on top of the closed basket, then dropped onto the bottom step.

Only then did he realize what he'd said. He set his plate next to hers and moved beside her. "I'm sorry. I shouldn't have said that. I wasn't trying to open old wounds."

"You didn't." She stared at her clasped hands in her

lap. "It's just that I don't think Dennis would have agreed with you."

"What do you mean?"

She drew in a deep breath before looking at him. "My marriage was a sham. Everybody thought Dennis and I were the perfect couple, but we were barely more than friends."

He could see the pain in her eyes and wished that he could make it go away. "Surely it wasn't always that way."

"No." She again looked at her hands as though she was too embarrassed to look at him. "I wouldn't have married him if it had been. But over time, his job took on a higher priority. He worked longer hours, and even when he was home, he was always tethered to his work."

Standing, she started to pace. "One day he announced that he wanted to move to Grand Junction. Said he could make more money there." She sighed. "Perhaps I should have heard him out. Instead, I told him no. We didn't need more money. That wasn't the real reason, though. Inside—" she laid a hand against her chest "—I kept thinking how lonely Megan and I would be in a strange place, not knowing anyone."

She stopped pacing then. "Dennis told me I was being selfish. That the only reason I didn't want to move was because I was afraid of change." Finally she met his gaze. "Then he slammed the door behind him. Two hours later, the police were at my door telling me he was dead."

Andrew's eyes fell closed as he processed her words. He understood just how she felt. He knew all too well what it was like to live with that kind of regret.

"Carly…" Standing, he wrapped his arms around her and pulled her against him, trying to decide who was the bigger jerk. Her husband for not giving his family the respect he should have, or him for bringing up the subject. "I'm so sorry."

She shook her head, tears falling. "I don't know. Maybe Dennis was right. Maybe I am afraid of change."

"Are you kidding?" Andrew set her away from him but still held onto her. "Look at how many changes you've not only faced but also overcome. You're a single mom, a business owner, and what about this fire?" He let go just long enough to gesture to the house. "You're stronger than you think, Carly. And you've tackled everything far better than most people."

"Thank you for saying that."

"I'm not just saying it. I know it."

Peering up at him, she smiled. "You need to eat before your food gets cold."

"Only if you'll join me."

She did, and as she started talking about her most recent phone call with Megan, he realized just how much grace this woman before him demonstrated under pressure. Like the night of the blizzard, when she climbed into a crumbling building to save those foals.

Carly was one in a million, all right. And he couldn't help wondering if she just might be the only one for him.

Chapter Sixteen

First thing Wednesday morning, Carly was busy in Livie's kitchen. Megan was on her way home, so her favorite foods were the order of the day. Peanut butter cookies with the chocolate Kiss in the middle, brownies, Carly's special four-cheese mac and cheese, and, tonight, Salisbury steak. Top that all off with the news that they'd be able to move back into Granger House on Friday and her daughter was going to be ecstatic. This would be a very good Good Friday.

Which reminded her, she needed to make some purchases. A new Easter dress for Megan. A ham. And probably some more replacement items for the kitchen. She'd ordered a lot of stuff online. Things that were now stored in Livie's laundry room. Then again, it had taken her a lifetime to collect all that kitchenware. She just hoped it didn't take that long to replace it.

Maybe they could run to Montrose tomorrow. Nothing better than a little retail therapy to kill time. Besides, Andrew would be too busy putting the finishing touches on things next door to spend a moment with them.

The thought of moving back into Granger House was a

bittersweet one, though. She'd soon be saying goodbye to Andrew. Too soon, as far as she was concerned.

I'd like you to help me keep Andrew in Ouray.

Lately she found herself wanting him to stay, too. If only she knew how to make Clint's—and her—wish come true.

She put the lid on the casserole dish and tucked the mac and cheese in the fridge for either lunch or a side with dinner tonight. She went through the motions of her chores, but Andrew was never far from her mind. No one except her parents had ever encouraged her the way Andrew did. Not even Dennis. Andrew listened to her and was honest with her, not simply placating her with what he thought she wanted to hear.

Like yesterday, when he pointed out all of the changes she'd actually faced and lived to tell about. She'd merely thought of it as overcoming what life threw her way. Perhaps he was right. Perhaps she was stronger than she thought.

With her baking complete, she scanned the functional yet less than appealing seventies-era kitchen. If she were to use this place as an extension of Granger House, the first thing she'd do was paint the dark wooden cabinets a lighter color. Maybe a light gray or white, like in her new kitchen. That would depend on the flooring, though. Given that the house was a hundred years old, she assumed there were hardwoods under this ugly vinyl. If that was the case, she'd have them refinished, perhaps even the same color Andrew used in the kitchen at Granger...

Oh, why was she wasting her time daydreaming? Because unless she could talk Andrew into selling her his half, it was pointless. And until she got the final bill for the repairs to Granger House, she wasn't even sure she could afford it.

She needed to focus on something productive while she waited for Megan.

Like Mona's scrapbooks. She'd already completed Noah's book and was ready to start on Andrew's.

She locked the back door and tilted the blinds so no one could see in before retrieving the stuff from the bedroom. The last thing she'd want was Andrew to come wandering in and spoil the surprise.

After laying out each small stack of photos, she found the handwritten note Mona had penned for her second-born. Did Carly dare look at it? No, not today. It would only make her cry.

She placed it back inside the box and began sorting the photos, putting them in chronological order. What a cute baby he was. And a mischievous-looking young boy. The next group of pictures was of his teen years. That playful gleam in his eyes wasn't nearly as prominent in his ninth grade school picture.

Shuffling to the next image, she smiled. What a handsome cowboy he was, though rather serious. She turned it over to read the note on the back.

Andrew, age 15. Working the ranch with Noah. My boys worked so hard to be men while their daddy was sick.

Carly flipped the picture back over and stared at the image. That was the summer of the horrible drought. His father had pneumonia then, too, as she recalled. Except it was much worse and included a lengthy stay in the hospital.

She and Andrew were only friends at that point, but close enough for her to know that he and Noah poured all their efforts into helping their parents that year. They'd not only done all of the work at the ranch but also spent the summer building fences for a rancher down the road who had offered to pay them. All in an effort to spare their parents the humiliation of having an adjoining piece of land they'd recently purchased foreclosed on by the bank.

In the end, the boys' hard work wasn't enough, and their parents lost that land anyway. She'd never forget the look on Andrew's face when he came to visit his grandmother shortly thereafter. He was so broken. That was probably when she'd first fallen in love with him.

The doorbell rang, jarring her from her thoughts.

She glanced at the starburst clock on the kitchen wall. Was it really almost noon? If so, then that would be her baby.

She set the stacks of photos in the box and tucked it back in the bedroom before rushing to open the front door to Megan and her grandparents.

"Oh, I'm so glad to see you." She hugged her daughter for all she was worth the moment she stepped inside.

"Mom, you're squishing me."

There was that word again. After five days apart, she would have thought she'd be Mommy once again.

Carly released her. "Guess what?"

"You made cookies? I can smell them."

"Yes, but that's not what I was going to tell you."

"Oh. Okay. What, then?" At least Megan's smile had an anticipatory air to it.

"We get to move back into Granger House on Friday."

The girl's eyes went wide. "Really?"

"Unless Andrew changes his mind."

Megan jumped up and down. "I can't wait to have my room back."

"Any chance we could see the finished product?" Beverly watched her with great expectation.

"I wish you could, but unfortunately, Andrew won't even let me see it. He's got the windows covered and everything. Says he wants to do one of those big reveals like they do on TV."

"He'll let me see it." Megan was too confident.

"Probably not. But you're welcome to try."

Her daughter started for the door.

"After you unpack your suitcase and have some lunch."

"Aw, man." Megan grabbed her suitcase and dragged it down the hall.

Chuck smiled at Carly. "We've heard a lot about this Andrew in recent days."

"Indeed." Beverly looked as though she was accusing her. "Seems Megan is quite taken with him."

"Andrew and I have known each other since we were kids. He's a good friend."

Beverly's brow arched. "A *very* good friend, according to Megan."

Carly loathed the heat she felt rising into her cheeks.

Her mother-in-law stepped closer then and took hold of her hands. "And that's okay."

What?

She jerked her gaze to Beverly's. The woman was smiling. Really smiling. At her, no less.

"Dennis has been gone for five years, Carly. It's time to move on."

Chuck came beside them, laying a hand on each of their shoulders. "We just want you and Megan to be happy."

A lump formed in Carly's throat. She could hardly believe the words she was hearing. Obviously she had misjudged the woman. Perhaps she should start thinking of her as a friend instead of her mother-in law.

She hugged both Wagners. "I appreciate that. But don't

worry." She looked at them now. "I have no plans to head to the altar anytime soon."

Andrew was still in shock. He never would have believed he could have put Carly's kitchen and family room back together in just four weeks. Yet by the grace of God, he'd managed to pull it off.

He was more than pleased with the way things had turned out. He'd even thrown in a few details she wasn't expecting. Now he couldn't wait to see her reaction.

"I didn't think this day would ever come." Carly moved through the front door of Granger House early Friday afternoon, hands clasped against her chest, a big smile on her beautiful face.

"It's so clean." Megan moved into the parlor, sniffing the air. "Smells clean, too."

"I know." Though she'd seen it before, Carly strolled through the space, examining everything from floor to ceiling. "I was skeptical when they said they'd be able to restore stuff to the way it was before the fire." Pausing, she bent over and sniffed one of the antique chairs, then straightened and smiled. "But they did a great job."

"I'm gonna check out my room." Megan ran across the wooden floor, taking a left at the dining room. "It smells good in here, too," she hollered a second later.

Shaking her head, Carly chuckled as she continued into the dining room, still taking in every nuance. "It's amazing how they were able to freshen everything."

Andrew stopped at the entrance to the kitchen. "Wait until you see what's in here."

Carly's smile had never been bigger. She practically wiggled with excitement as she approached.

"Don't you want to wait for Megan?"

"Megan," she called over her shoulder. "Hurry up so we can see our new kitchen."

"Coming." Her daughter was at her side in no time, both of them looking up at Andrew with those blue eyes filled with anticipation.

"Are you ladies ready to see your new kitchen and family room?"

"Yes," they responded collectively.

"You're sure?"

"Andrew…" Carly ground out the word.

"Okay, okay." Having replaced the old swinging door with a more practical pocket door, he slid it aside, allowing them to enter. "Welcome home."

Just like on those HGTV shows, Carly gasped, her eyes going wide as her hands moved to her mouth.

"Whoa…" Megan moved across the newly refinished floors, turning in circles.

Continuing toward the large island, Carly looked left, right, up and down as if trying to take it all in. "Is this really mine?" She touched the apron-front sink.

"Yep." Watching her, seeing her so happy, filled his heart to overflowing.

Megan climbed onto one of the high-backed stools that sat along the far side of the island. "This is the best kitchen ever." She laid her cheek against the marble, her arms spreading across the expanse as though she were hugging it.

"It's so much brighter." Walking between the island and the stove, Carly smoothed a hand across the marble. Suddenly she stopped and whirled to face him. "Glass knobs? I told you I couldn't afford them."

"I know. But you wanted them." Hands shoved in his pockets, he rocked back on his heels. "My way of saying thank you for all the help you gave us at the ranch."

She opened her mouth slightly, then closed it without saying a word. She didn't need to, though. The tears welling her in eyes said it all.

"What's that?" Megan hopped down from the stool and hurried to the far corner of the room.

"That's your mom's new pantry." He moved beside Carly, gesturing toward her daughter. "Let's check it out."

Megan opened the door and moved inside. "This is so cool."

"I love the door." Carly caressed the frosted glass that read Pantry as they passed. She poked her head inside. "Holy cow." She looked back at him now. "I can't believe all this storage."

"I know. And all we did was utilize a corner that had been wasted space anyway."

Smiling, she said, "How did you get so smart?"

"It's a gift."

Megan squeezed past her mother. "Hey, cool table." She dodged toward his other surprise, positioned near the opening to the family room, beside the wall where the stove had once been.

Placing his hand against the small of Carly's back, he urged her that way.

Her eyes grew bigger with every step. "Is that what I think it is?"

He nodded. "It took forever, but I was able to sand down the old butcher block to use as the tabletop, and Jude turned the legs for me." He looked at Carly now. "He's quite the woodworker. And his specialty is custom millwork. He helped me with some of the window casings that were damaged."

"So that's why you kept telling me to stay away from the shop while you were hanging out at the ranch, waiting for the floors to dry." She fingered the satin finish.

"This butcher block was one of the original countertops in Granger House."

"I remembered you saying that. Which is why I couldn't let it go to waste."

She reached for his hand, entwining their fingers. "I can't tell you how much I appreciate this. The table, the knobs, everything. This kitchen exceeds my wildest dreams, Andrew. And I'm glad it was you who made them come true." Pushing up on her toes, she kissed his cheek. "Thank you."

He stared into her blue eyes brimming with gratitude. He longed to take her into his arms and tell her how he felt. That he loved her. But considering Megan was here, he should probably wait.

Instead, he gently cupped Carly's cheek. "I'm glad I was here to do it. However—" He tugged her toward the family room. "There's more to see."

He led them into the cozy space with its warm gray walls, white-slipcovered furniture and natural wood entertainment center that surrounded their new 55-inch flat screen TV.

"This looks like something out of a magazine." Carly continued into the space. "I love the wood accents."

"The TV is huge!" Megan rushed to the opposite side of the room and picked up the remote. "Can I turn it on?"

"Not yet." Carly started back toward the kitchen. "We still have plenty of work to do."

After a little more exploring, they headed back to his grandmother's to gather their things.

He picked up a box from the kitchen counter that contained several shoe boxes. "What's this?"

"Oh!" Carly immediately turned away from the groceries she'd been bagging, hurried toward him and intercepted the box. "It's nothing you'd be interested in."

Then why did she look so sheepish?

"Why don't you take some of the heavier stuff I stored in the laundry room? Like my new pots and pans and that pretty purple stand mixer." Lately it seemed a day hadn't gone by without a deliveryman showing up at his grand-mother's door or Carly running to Montrose to pick up replacement items for those she'd lost in the fire. Nothing like giving a woman a reason to shop.

"Purple, huh?" He opened the door to the laundry room off his grandmother's kitchen. "Let me guess. Megan picked it out."

Carly smiled over the box she was still holding. "Yes. I think it'll be a nice pop of color in my new kitchen."

They trudged back and forth between the two houses for the next couple of hours until they'd gotten everything.

"I don't know about you two, but I'm famished." He dropped the final box on the kitchen counter. "What do you ladies say I go grab us some pizza?"

"Pizza?" Who knew it was so easy to get Megan's at-tention? "Can we?" She deferred to her mother.

Carly glanced around the space that was now brim-ming with bags and boxes of all kinds. "I don't think I'll be doing any cooking tonight, so go for it."

They ate at her new table, and later, after Megan had gone to bed and he convinced Carly she didn't have to unpack everything tonight, the two of them sat down on her comfy new sofa.

"It all feels so new." She snuggled beside him as he put his arm around her. "Like it's a brand-new house."

"In many ways, it is. New walls, new flooring, new furniture…"

"I love the glass knobs." She peered up at him, her smile making him want to do even more for her. "And you said I was spoiling you."

He chuckled. "You haven't gotten my bill yet."

She playfully swatted him.

"Seriously, though, I'm not going to charge you for any labor."

"Wha—?" She twisted to face him. "That's crazy. Why would you do that?"

"After all you've done for us? Helping with Dad and the foals. You gave up your day-to-day life. I think it's a pretty fair trade."

Brow furrowing, she seemed to ponder his words. "I'm not so sure about that. I mean, how would I have gotten through this craziness without you? The fire, redoing the kitchen… It was all so overwhelming."

He touched her cheek with the back of his hand. "I'm glad God put me in Ouray when He did."

There was that smile again. "Me, too."

Threading his fingers into her curls, he drew her closer. Breathed in the tropical scent of her shampoo, staring into her eyes for a moment and seeing eternity. The life he wanted. A life he wanted with her. She was the only woman he'd ever loved. The only one he could imagine giving his heart to. And boy, did she have it. Lowering his head, he claimed her lips. Tasted the spiciness of pizza, the sweetness of forever. He didn't know he was capable of loving one person so much.

But he did. And there was only one thing he could do about it.

Talk Carly into coming to Denver with him.

Chapter Seventeen

Carly never imagined there would be so much to do by simply moving back into her own home. But while most of Granger House remained the same, the heart of it, the kitchen and family room, was a complete do-over. Even the simplest things were gone, and it hadn't crossed her mind to add them to her inventory list. Things like a paper towel holder, dishrags and containers to hold flour and sugar. Probably because she'd had those things at Livie's house. Whatever the case, she was looking at either another shopping trip or more boxes arriving at her door.

For now, she'd started a list. Something that was likely to be ongoing as she worked to make her house a home again and an inviting retreat for guests.

Taking a sip of her second cup of tea from the Adventures in Pink Jeep Tours mug Blakely had given her from her tour company, she leaned back in one of the padded bar stools at her delightfully large island and admired her new kitchen. Yet as magnificent as it was, it couldn't dim the memory of Andrew and his kiss. *His* kiss.

Looking back, she sheepishly realized that she was the one who'd made the first move when they'd kissed before.

But not last night. That was a curl-your-toes, make-you-sigh kind of kiss.

The mere memory had her cheeks warming.

Banishing the wayward thoughts from her mind, she focused on today. Since tomorrow was Easter, this was the perfect opportunity to break in her new stove. She'd have to boil some eggs to be colored later, decide on and make the dessert—maybe a fluffy coconut cake—and bake the ham. Even though she still had plenty to get back in order before she could host any B and B guests, she'd invited the Stephens men to join her and Megan for dinner tomorrow. Plus it would give Andrew the opportunity to show them all what he'd been working on this past month.

A few silent moments later, she discovered the best thing about sitting at her new island. From this vantage point, she was able to catch that first glimpse of her sleepy-headed daughter as she shuffled into the kitchen in her pajamas, rubbing her eyes, unaware that anyone was watching her. Like when Megan was a toddler. Only her blankie was missing.

"Good morning, sweetie." She hugged Megan, assisting her as she climbed onto the next stool.

"Morning." She yawned. "What's for breakfast?"

"I don't know. Cereal, may—"

A knock sounded at the back door.

Turning, she saw Andrew on the other side, waving.

"Anybody in the mood for some hot, fresh cinnamon rolls?" he asked as she swung open the door.

She glanced back at Megan. "Guess that answers your question."

Carly pulled three new plates and forks from the dishwasher and set them on the other side of the island as Andrew served up the rolls.

Finished, he licked the icing from his fingers. "There's

a great doughnut shop just down the street from my place in Denver. Their doughnuts are so light and fluffy they practically melt in your mouth."

"I like doughnuts." Megan turned to Carly. "Don't you, Mommy?"

"On occasion. I much prefer one of Celeste's cinnamon rolls, though."

After breakfast, while she cleared off the island and counters on either side of the stove so she could start cooking, Andrew brought in the boxes from the garage. Items they'd salvaged from the fire, things like casserole dishes and cast iron skillets, as well as other belongings that had been stored there while the house was being worked on.

"You know, since reworking your kitchen—" he dropped another box on the long counter in front of the window "—I've been thinking about expanding Magnum Custom Homes."

"That's your new company, right?" She filled the large pot with enough water to cover the eggs and set it on the stove.

"Yes." He grinned. "Or will be in a few days, anyway." Approaching the island, he continued. "But what if someone doesn't necessarily want a new home? What if they just want to improve the one they're in?"

Eyeing two glass casseroles that needed to go into the dishwasher, she crossed to get them. "Like remodeling?"

"Sort of. But we're talking luxury homes—" his eyes followed her as she returned to the sink "—so let's call it…reimagining."

"Catchy." She added the items to the dishwasher.

"Right? So what if, in addition to new homes, we offer custom redesigns to help people *reimagine* the home they're in? And we wouldn't limit ourselves to just kitchens and baths. Not when there's so much more out there. Theater rooms and outdoor spaces are hot right now."

She closed the door to the machine, giving him her full attention. "Sounds like a good way to increase business."

"I know it'll take time to get things up to speed and on the path to growth, but I'm used to that. Trying new things is part of the freedom that comes with owning my own business."

"Kind of like when I try a new recipe for the B and B?"

"That's right. If they work, great. If not—" he shrugged "—we move on to the next idea. That's how I was able to grow Pinnacle Construction so quickly. I kept challenging myself to do things better than the other guy." The excitement in his voice had her feeling somewhat dismayed.

Listening to him, she realized how little she really knew about his world outside Ouray. He wasn't some small-town builder. He'd grown a major construction company from the ground up and then sold it for more money than she could imagine.

And hearing him now, she had no doubt he would put every bit as much of himself into this new business. Leaving little time for anything else.

An ache filled her heart. Which was foolish. There were no promises between her and Andrew. No commitment. She knew all along he'd be leaving.

As the day progressed, she tried not to think too much about that aspect of things and simply focused on her house and savoring what time she and Megan had left with him. They all colored Easter eggs, each of them trying to outdo the other two when it came to color and style. She genuinely enjoyed Andrew's company and the way he made her feel as though she could do anything.

Yet the more he talked about Denver and all it had to offer, the more she realized how much she'd come to hope he would stay. But that wasn't going to happen. No matter how badly she and Clint wanted it to.

For the second night in a row, Andrew joined her on the couch in the family room after Megan went to bed. Though for Carly, things didn't feel near as cozy as they had last night.

"You know, I'm going to have to leave Monday to head back to Denver," he said.

She nodded, not wanting to face reality. Why had she allowed herself to believe that maybe this was their second chance?

Taking hold of her hand, he faced her. "These weeks with you have reminded me how good life can be." His dark gaze bore into hers. "I don't want to lose that."

Her heart leaped for joy, excitement spreading through her entire body. This connection between them hadn't been all in her mind. He felt it, too.

He looked at their entwined fingers, his thumb caressing the back of her hand, before he smiled at her. "I'd like you to come to Denver with me. You and Megan."

Just as quickly as her spirits had taken flight, they crashed and burned.

Did he even realize what he was asking? What about Granger House? What about Megan's school? She couldn't just uproot her, take her away from everything she'd ever known.

She thought back to that first and only semester she'd spent in Denver. All those lonely nights in her dorm room while Andrew worked. He said he was saving for their future. What kind of future could they have if they were never together?

None.

I know it'll take time to get things up to speed and on the path to growth, but I'm used to that.

Andrew might be used to devoting himself to his work, but where did that leave her and Megan?

Playing second fiddle, that's where. Just like they had with Dennis. And she'd vowed she would never put herself or her daughter through that again.

Slowly withdrawing her hand from his, she tried hard to keep the tears that threatened from falling. "I'm sorry. I—I can't do that."

He looked confused at first. Then upset. "Can't or won't?"

"Andrew, running your business is your top priority."

"Of course it is. It has to be."

"And I get that. But what about my business? Granger House is important to me."

His gaze searched hers. "But, I—" He shook his head. "Then where does that leave us?"

God, give me strength.

"There is no us." She stood, unable to look at him for fear she'd break down and cry. "We're too different, Andrew. You're driven to succeed. And I refuse to take second place in someone's life ever again."

He was silent for a long time, just sitting there with his forearms resting on his thighs, his head hung low. She'd hurt him. But what was she supposed to do? He hadn't even said he loved her.

"I guess it's time for me to go, then," he finally said.

She drew in a deep breath as he stood. "I'll walk you out."

They moved silently through the house and out onto the front porch. The night air was unusually warm, but she was chilled nonetheless. Still, there was one more thing they needed to discuss.

"So, what are we going to do about your grandmother's?"

"I told you, I'm not selling, Carly. Not to you or anyone else. However, my offer still stands, if you'd like to reconsider."

"But that would mean giving up my dream of expanding."

He shrugged. "The choice is yours." He stared at her for what seemed like forever. There in those eyes she loved so much, she could see her own pain reflected.

Then, as though resigning himself, his body drooped. He stepped toward her, cupped her right cheek, then kissed the other. "You're the only woman I've ever loved." His words were a whisper on her ear, but they echoed through her heart and mind like an agonizing shout. He did love her. It didn't matter, though. He'd made his decision.

"Goodbye, Carly."

Arms crossed over her chest, she managed to keep her feet riveted to the porch until he pulled out of the drive. Once he was out of sight, she hurried inside, collapsed on her bed and cried until she fell asleep.

The first time Andrew lost Carly, he started Pinnacle Construction and threw himself into his work. When Mama died, he was too busy living his dream to be there to tell her goodbye. The ache of what he'd done nearly killed him. Instead of pulling back, though, he worked even harder, trying desperately to forget. But it was impossible.

Then Crawford Construction made him an offer. He figured God was trying to tell him something. To slow down. So he came back to Ouray and, for the first time, experienced firsthand all that his life had been missing.

Now here he was again, about to embark on a new business with a busted-up heart throbbing in his chest.

Driving back to the ranch, he swallowed the bitter taste stinging the back of his throat. He'd wanted to argue his case against Carly's protests. Yes, he was driven. Yes, he was a hard worker. But he wasn't her late husband. And if there's one thing he'd learned, it was how important family was to him. He'd never squander that.

Yet he'd heard the pain in her voice, seen it in her eyes, when she talked about her marriage that day over lunch. He could have made her all the promises in the world tonight and she still wouldn't have believed him.

He needed to get away from Ouray. Go back to Denver, close the deal with Magnum, throw himself into his work and forget about love, because it obviously wasn't meant for him.

When he pulled up to the ranch house, there was a white SUV parked beside his father's dually. What would Hillary be doing here this time of night? It was almost ten o'clock.

He heard laughter coming from the kitchen as he entered the mudroom. Following the voices, he spotted his father and Hillary sitting at the kitchen table.

If he was quiet and kept moving, they'd never notice him.

He started through the family room.

"Hello, Andrew," said Hillary.

He cringed.

"Pull up a chair and join us, son." Dad scraped the wooden chair closest to him across the vinyl floor.

The last thing Andrew was in the mood for was conversation. Though he was staring. While he knew there was nothing romantic going on, seeing his father sitting across the table from a woman other than Mama was downright strange.

"I had dinner at Granny's Kitchen tonight," Dad continued, as though he'd read Andrew's mind. "Ran into Hillary, so we decided to come back here for some coffee."

"Thanks, Dad, but I'm going to go pack. I need to leave in the morning."

"In the morning? But it's Easter. We're supposed to have dinner at Carly's." His father stood, his voice holding both surprise and disappointment. "Are you sure this is what you want to do, son?"

"Yes, sir." If only his heart was as certain as his head.

"Did the two of you decide what you're going to do about Livie's house?"

"No. No decision yet." He could only pray Carly would accept his offer, because as long as they both owned that house, they'd be connected. And right now, he wasn't sure he could handle that.

"You like living in Denver?" Hillary peered at him over the rim of her coffee cup.

"Yes, ma'am. I've built one successful business and am about to close on another. Guess you'd say I'm living my dream." At least that's what he used to think. Until Carly came back into his life.

"Or having fun chasing them, anyway." She smiled.

Had he heard her correctly? "I'm sorry. What?"

She stood now, rounded the table. "I was like you. Growing up, I couldn't wait to get out of Ouray. Vowed I'd never come back." Arms crossed, she leaned against the counter. "I wanted to travel the world and be somebody. You know? Successful. And that's exactly what I did."

"Oh. I guess I was under the impression that you lived in Ouray."

"I do. Now. But I should have done it a lot sooner. I was just too hardheaded and stubborn."

"You, stubborn?" His father sent her a curious look.

"Oh, you hush, Clint." She turned her attention back to Andrew. "I had a beautiful home, a nice car, expensive clothes and more money than I could possibly spend. But I was alone. And it was the pits."

Why was she telling him this? He glanced at his father. Or, what had Dad been telling her?

"Well, I'm glad you're here now, Hillary." He pointed toward his father. "This guy needs a good sparring partner."

After bidding them good-night, he went to Daniel's room and closed the door, grateful his brother was nowhere to be found. He didn't feel like talking. Yet as he crawled into the second of the two twin beds, sleep evaded him.

But what about my business? Granger House is important to me.

He understood Carly's commitment. It's one of the things he admired about her. But his hands were tied with Magnum. He was contractually obligated to move forward with the purchase or risk being sued. Leaving him no choice but to go back to Denver. No matter how much he wished he could stay.

He tossed and turned most of the night, thoughts of Carly plaguing his mind. By morning, he knew what he had to do.

He said goodbye to his father then headed into town before the sun topped the Amphitheater, the curved volcanic formation on Ouray's eastern edge. While daylight invaded the sky, Ouray would remain bathed in shadows until the sun topped the mountain almost an hour from now.

Pulling into his grandmother's drive, he couldn't take his eyes off Granger House. From here he could see through Carly's kitchen window. The two pendant lights over the island glowed, telling him she was awake.

He drew in a deep breath as he exited his truck and

made his way to her back door. *God, I know this is the right thing to do. Just please help me do it.*

He climbed the few steps and gently knocked on the door.

When it opened a moment later, Carly stood there in her fuzzy robe, mug in hand, her curls going every which way. She was the most beautiful woman he'd ever seen. What he wouldn't have given to wake up to that every morning.

But that wasn't going to happen.

"Andrew." She ran a self-conscious hand through her hair.

"I'm on my way back to Denver. But there's something I need to talk to you about."

"Okay." She moved out of the way, holding the door so he could enter.

He took in the space he'd worked so hard on, hoping to make Carly's dreams come true. And he believed he had. If only he could be a part of those dreams.

"I won't keep you," he said. "I just wanted to let you know that I'm giving you my half of my grandmother's house."

Her blue eyes went wide.

"You can do with it as you please. Renovate it, use it for the B and B or whatever, with the stipulation that if you ever decide you no longer want it, you will give me back my half and let me purchase yours."

"Wow. That's…that's very generous of you. But…why?"

He gazed at her, unable to deny the longing in his heart. "Because I can't think of anyone who would take better care of it."

She smiled now, but not the big, vivacious sort he was used to seeing. This one was more tentative. Sad, even. The kind that made him want to wrap his arms around her and tell her everything would be okay.

"I promise I will. Thank you."

"I'll have my attorney draw up the papers and get them to you as soon as possible."

She nodded, looking as though she wanted to say something more. When she didn't—

"I need to be going." He turned for the door.

"Andrew?"

He turned back, his heart hopeful.

She hesitated a moment. Then— "Drive safely."

He forced a smile, wondering if he'd ever see her again. "I will."

Chapter Eighteen

For the second time in less than twelve hours, Carly watched Andrew pull out of the drive. He was gone. Forever.

She missed him already.

Still, she'd made the right choice, hadn't she? After all, he'd even said that his business was his top priority. Not her, not family. Business. She couldn't live like that again. Watching their relationship dissolve into nothing. Her heart wouldn't be able to take it.

Despite everything, though, he'd given her his half of Livie's house. Making her dream of expanding Granger House Inn possible. So why wasn't she jumping up and down, cheering at the top of her lungs? Wasn't that what she'd wanted all along? Where was the excitement?

Gone with Andrew.

Though he'd never even been a part of the equation, without him, turning Livie's house into an extension of the B and B just didn't feel right.

She downed what remained of her lukewarm tea and set the mug on the island beside the pretty basket containing the colorful eggs they'd decorated. After crying much of the night, she must look like a mess.

She went into her bedroom, knowing she needed to get ready for church. She looked at herself in her bathroom mirror. Puffy, red eyes stared back at her. No wonder Andrew had been so eager to leave.

Turning, she slumped against the vanity. Who was she trying to kid? He left because there was nothing more to say. Their relationship was over. And still he'd given her his half of Livie's house. A move that made her love him all the more.

Tears threatened again, but she blinked them away. Tea. She needed more tea.

Returning to the kitchen, she grabbed another tea bag from the box on the counter, put it in her mug, added some water and put the cup in the microwave. She still couldn't believe she'd forgotten to buy a kettle. Since there was one at Livie's, it had completely slipped her mind. Add that to her ever-growing list of items that needed to be replaced.

Perhaps she should make a run into Montrose tomorrow and see what she could pick up. Hanging out in her new kitchen would only make her think of Andrew. She needed something to distract her. At least for a while.

She glanced at the clock. Almost eight o'clock and still no sign of Megan. She must be worn out from helping them yesterday. Unpacking, moving stuff around in her room.

Mug in hand, Carly moved to the beautiful table Andrew had made her out of the old butcher block. She smoothed her palm over the satiny surface. What a fun surprise this had been. Her gaze shifted to the family room before taking in the kitchen once again. Memories of Andrew seemed to be everywhere she looked.

She eyed the cardboard container of scrapbooks and shoe boxes she'd tucked in one of the four chairs. Whether Andrew was in her life or not, she would still complete them. She'd made a promise to both Clint and Mona.

She placed her cup on the table and picked up the shoe box belonging to Andrew. She knew it was foolish. Why torture herself?

But that wasn't enough to stop her from lifting the lid. There, on top, was the note Mona had written.

Carly picked it up, more curious than ever. What had Mona wanted to say to her second-born son? And though she knew she shouldn't look, Carly desperately wanted to know.

She fingered open the flap on the envelope, pulled out the note card adorned with columbines and read.

My sweet Andrew,
You were always my ambitious one. And so much like your father. You work hard and love even harder. Some think you're a workaholic. Inside, though, you long to be a family man. Or did, anyway. Until your heart was broken.

Carly's hand went to her mouth. Was Mona referring to her? Was she the one who broke Andrew's heart?

Instead of dusting yourself off and moving on, you channeled all of your energy and passion into your business, and it's paid off. But a mother longs to see her children happy. And despite your success, I don't believe you are.

An image of Andrew sprang to her mind. That day six weeks ago when she first saw him at Livie's. He was so intense. Not at all like the man she once knew. Or the man he'd been these past weeks.

Andrew, I pray that you will one day find the strength to let go of the pain of the past and allow yourself to love again. Open your heart to the future God has planned for you. You never know where it may lead.

A tear trailed down Carly's cheek. How could she have been so stupid? Andrew was the kind of man she'd always wanted. Yet she'd let him walk out of her life. Not just once, but twice. All because she was afraid.

Andrew was not Dennis. He'd demonstrated more love and understanding in this past month than she'd experienced in most of her marriage. Andrew went out of his way to show how much he cared for both her and Megan. Like that day he took her to the movies in Montrose and that first night when he taught Megan to play cards.

She tucked Mona's card back into the envelope and set it inside the box, her fingers brushing that photo of Andrew at fifteen. She picked it up. "Oh, Andrew, I do love you."

Enough to leave Ouray and risk a future with him in Denver?

Smiling, she swiped another tear from her face. Mona was right. It was time to let go of the past and see what God had planned for her future. To do that, though, she had to find Andrew.

But how? It wasn't like she could just call him and say, "I've had a change of heart. Would you mind turning around?" No, she had to prove she loved him and was committed to their relationship, no matter where they lived. That meant she had to go to him.

She hurried into her bedroom, threw on a pair of jeans and a sweater, then gathered a few things and threw them into her tote. Clint would know where she could find him. Where he lived. She and Megan could stop by the ranch on their way out of town.

Finished, she set her bag by the back door and went into Megan's room. "Wake up, baby. We need to—"

Megan's bed was empty.

"Megan!" she hollered as she left her daughter's bedroom, then again as she headed into the family room. Where could she be?

She searched the kitchen, her bedroom, the dining room and the parlor before heading upstairs. "Megan!"

Her sweaty palms skimmed across the banister as panic rose in her gut. She'd heard of children being taken from their beds, never to be seen again.

Finding nothing in the three bedrooms upstairs, she rushed back downstairs and searched Megan's room for any sign of foul play, any hint where her daughter could have gone. The windows were still locked with the blinds closed, and nothing was out of place.

"Megan!"

She went to the front door. It was unlocked and ajar.

Her heart sank into her stomach. She always locked up at night.

Pushing through the storm door, she checked the porch. "Megan?"

The silence reverberated in her ears.

She glanced left, then right. Spotting Livie's house, she darted down the steps. Maybe Megan forgot something and had gone back to retrieve it. She tried the front door. Locked. She rushed to the back. Locked again.

The key. She needed the key.

She hurried across the drive, into the kitchen, grabbed the key and went back to Livie's. Pushed through the back door. "Megan?"

She searched this house, too, her anxiety ratcheting up a notch with every empty room. Her stomach churned, her breaths coming so quickly she was getting light-headed. Where was she?

God, help me.

Pulling her cell phone from her pocket, she dialed 911 and choked back the tears that threatened to consume her.

"Ouray 9—"

"My daughter's missing."

Andrew continued north on Highway 550 on his way back to Denver, staring out over the open range without ever really seeing anything. When he'd arrived in Ouray almost five weeks ago, his plan had been to do the renovations at his grandmother's house as quickly as possible and then move on down the road with the possibility of some rental income. But all that changed when Carly walked in.

Now he wasn't sure if his life would ever be the same. If he'd ever be the same. Because for the first time in his adult life, he wasn't thinking about sales numbers or the next big deal. All he could think about was Carly. What was she doing? Was she already planning what to do with his grandmother's house, or was she sitting there with her cup of tea, missing him, too? And had she tamed those wayward curls?

The thought made him smile.

He was halfway to Montrose when he'd reigned in his emotions enough to call his attorney. So what if it was Easter? Ned would understand. He pressed the button on his steering wheel for the hands-free calling feature.

"Call Ned." The sooner they got the legalities squared away, the sooner Carly could incorporate his grandmother's house into the B and B.

"Hey, buddy." Ned's voice boomed through the speakers.

"I need you to do something for me." He went over what he wanted.

"Sure. Since you're both in agreement, it shouldn't take long at all. So, are you looking forward to getting back to the real world again?"

Strangely, he found life to be more real in Ouray than it had ever been in Denver. Between the fire, the foals, his dad and the blizzard, it had been an eventful few weeks. "I suppose."

"You don't sound very excited."

"Let's just say things in Denver don't hold the same allure as they once did."

"I see. This sudden change of heart wouldn't have anything to do with this Carly person, would it?"

He blew out a breath. "She helped me to see how much of life I've been missing out on."

"Then why are you leaving us?"

Andrew jerked his head toward the backseat, causing his vehicle to swerve.

"Megan?" He overcorrected, veering into the other lane.

A horn sounded from an oncoming car.

"What's going on, Andrew?" Ned asked through the speaker.

Heart pounding, Andrew put on his blinker and eased onto the shoulder. "I'll call you back, Ned." He ended the call and turned around.

"Megan, what are you doing here?" The poor kid was crying. No wonder. He could have killed them both. "Does your mother know where you are?"

"No." Shaking her head, she tearfully climbed over the leather console and into the passenger seat. Only then did he realize she was still wearing her pajamas.

He willed his heart rate to a normal rhythm. "Okay, sweetheart, what gives?"

"You can't leave us." Her bottom lip quivered.

"I don't have a choice, Megan."

"Yes, you do!" she yelled. "We love you and I know you love us, too."

He let go a sigh. Out of the mouths of babes.

Even Megan got it. How come he didn't?

Because until recently, all of his hopes and dreams had been in Denver.

He eyed the child he'd grown to love. Could God have put her here for a reason?

Yeah, to show him what a giant mistake he was making.

"Come here." He took the sobbing girl into his arms, feeling like the biggest jerk in the world. He couldn't have cared for her more if she were his own daughter. He wanted to watch her grow, to teach her how to drive and protect her from all those dates she was bound to have in a few years.

Most of all, he didn't want to go through life alone anymore. Hillary was right. It was the pits. He wanted to be closer to his father and brothers. And he wanted to be with Carly and Megan. Maybe Colorado's western slope was in need of a good construction/remodeling company.

Whatever the case, he knew in his heart that staying in Ouray was not only the right thing to do but also what God had been trying to tell him the entire time he was there. *Thank You, Lord.*

When Megan had calmed down, he set her away from him. "You're a pretty perceptive kid, you know that?"

"What does that mean?" She sniffed.

Lifting the lid on the console, he pulled out a napkin and handed it to her. "It means that you're right. I do love you. And your mama, too." Except he hadn't told Carly until he'd been walking away. What kind of guy did that?

His cell rang then, his dad's name appearing on the dashboard screen.

He pressed the button on the steering wheel to answer. "What's up, Dad?"

"Jude just called. Megan is missing."

Megan's eyes were wide as she looked up at him.

"I'm on my way to—"

"She's with me, Dad."

"Megan?"

"Yes." He continued to watch a silent, perhaps terrified, Megan. "Tell Carly not to worry. We'll be there shortly to explain."

"I wasn't trying to make Mommy sad," she said as he ended the call. "I just wanted—"

He touched her cheek. "I know. Now buckle up." He waited for the traffic to clear, then made a U-turn and headed back toward Ouray. "We don't want to be late for Easter service."

When they arrived at Carly's, she was out of the house and in the drive with his dad and Jude right behind her before he brought the truck to a stop.

She opened the passenger door and scooped her daughter into her arms. "Baby, you scared me to death. What were you thinking?"

Megan didn't respond. She simply twisted her head to look at him as he rounded the front of the vehicle.

He looked at Carly now. He could tell she'd been crying. Still, she was beautiful. Why had he ever thought he could walk away from her again?

"Would you guys mind taking Megan into the house while I talk to Carly?"

"Not a problem," said his brother, already making his departure.

"Come on, darlin'." The old man held out his hand as

Carly set Megan on the ground. A few moments later, the three of them disappeared into the kitchen.

"Thank you for bringing her back." Carly crossed her arms over her chest. "But I don't understand how she ended up with you in the first place."

"She stowed away in my truck."

"What?" Her brow puckered. "Why would she do that?"

"Megan said she overheard us talking last night and then again this morning."

Carly winced, the morning breeze gently tossing those crazy curls of hers.

"Let's just say she thought I needed a little friendly advice."

Carly's mouth twitched, her arms dropping to her sides. "I'm sorry she caused you so much trouble."

He took a step closer. "She wasn't any trouble. At least, not once I got the truck under control again."

"Oh, no." She did smile then.

"Hey, we're both in one piece, and she's home safe and sound."

Carly nodded but wouldn't look at him.

So he forced her to do just that by erasing what little space remained between them and touching a finger to her chin. To his surprise, she didn't pull away.

"I love you, Carly. And I love your daughter, too."

Her body relaxed as though she was relieved. Then she laid a hand to his chest, staring up at him with those blue eyes. "I love you, too. And I'm willing to go to Denver or anywhere else with you, if you still want me to."

Being with her was what he wanted more than anything. But hearing her say those words made him realize how selfish he was even to have asked. She had built a successful business here, and she was an integral part of the community. A community he'd grown to care about a great deal these past few weeks.

Shaking his head ever so slightly, he slid his arms around her waist. "I don't belong in Denver. Ouray is my home, and home is where I need to be."

"What about Magnum Homes?"

"I'm still bound to the purchase. However, I might have to see about getting someone else to run it, because I plan to spend my time here with you."

Lowering his head, he kissed her. This amazing woman who had taught him more about himself than he'd ever known. She was his past, his present and his future.

Still holding her, he looked into the eyes of the woman he loved. "I guess we'd better get ready for church." He stroked her arms. "After all, Easter is a time of renewal and new beginnings."

"A new kitchen, new directions…"

"New life." He smiled, pulling her to him once again. "I guess my parents named the ranch correctly after all. Because I am abundantly blessed, indeed."

Epilogue

Carly couldn't think of any better time than Mother's Day to give the Stephens brothers the scrapbooks their mother had so lovingly planned for them. Mona was an amazing woman who'd raised five wonderful sons, and she deserved to be celebrated.

Of course, the guys didn't know anything about the scrapbooks. They simply thought they were treating Carly to lunch at the ranch because, as Andrew told her, "You're a mom, so it's our turn to celebrate you."

A day at the ranch would be a nice break. Since its reopening, Granger House Inn had enjoyed two fully booked weekends in a row, and she already had bookings all the way into August. By the time Andrew finished the renovations at Livie's house later this summer and they started hosting guests there, this could end up being one of the B and B's best years ever.

With her guests checked out by noon and the kitchen clean, she packaged up some of the leftover lemon cheesecake tarts and fudgy hazelnut cream cookies and headed out to the ranch. She knew the guys would have plenty of good food, but they always appreciated her leftovers. Especially the sweets.

Andrew had picked Megan up earlier from church and brought her back with him. Carly had a suspicion they were working on a surprise of their own. It was Mother's Day, after all.

Turning into the ranch, she noticed a dark gray Jeep pulling in behind her. Another glance in her rearview mirror revealed the driver as the third Stephens boy, Matt.

It had been a while since Carly had a chance to talk with him. She'd seen him in passing around town, but according to Andrew, Matt tended to steer clear of the ranch due to a strained relationship with his father. However, he was here, which meant he'd at least responded to Clint's request.

"Long time, no see," she said when they simultaneously emerged from their vehicles in front of the ranch house.

Matt, who was a couple of years younger than her, smiled as he came toward her. Like Noah, Andrew and Jude, he had the same dark hair and eyes as their father, though she could see a little Mona in him, too. His nose and the shape of his mouth definitely belonged to his mother.

"Sheriff's been working me too hard." He hugged her. "Good to see you, Carly." Releasing her, he nodded in the direction of the new barn. "Looks like Andrew's making some headway."

"Are you kidding? That's been his top priority." In the five weeks since Magnum Homes' owner's son backed out at the closing, deciding he couldn't let go of his father's legacy, Andrew had devoted most of his time to clearing away the old barn and starting the framework on the new. That is, between weekend trips to Denver to empty out his house so he could put it on the market.

"Well, we were long overdue for a new one."

She laid a hand on his shoulder. "I hear you're pretty good with a hammer. I'm sure he'd welcome the help."

He stared down at her. Nodded. "I'll think about it."

"Good." At least he hadn't said no. "Mind helping me carry in some stuff?"

"Not at all."

She opened the back door of her SUV and pointed to the large box that contained all five of the gift-bagged scrapbooks. To ensure there would be no peeking, she'd not only closed the flaps on the box but also sealed it with packing tape.

"This it?" he asked, hoisting the box into his capable arms.

"Yes, sir. Just let me grab these desserts and we'll head inside."

"Sweets, you say? That sounds promising."

She closed the passenger door and started up the steps of the deck. "One of the perks of owning a bed-and-breakfast. I almost always have sweets on hand." As she opened the door to the mudroom, it dawned on her that Matt lived only a couple of blocks from her. "You know, I'm always trying out new recipes. Would you mind if I dropped some samples by your place?"

"Mind? Carly, you're talking to a bachelor. We never turn down food."

She could hear a bustle of activity coming from the kitchen as soon as they stepped inside.

"No. The fork goes on the left and the knife goes on the right." Megan was giving somebody orders.

Matt looked at her over his shoulder. "Where would you like me to put this?"

"Anywhere in the family room is fine."

A lunch of prime rib, twice-baked potatoes and broccoli exceeded anything Carly might have anticipated. Given that they were cattle ranchers, she'd come to expect beef, but prime rib was definitely a special treat. And this one was cooked to perfection.

In addition to the meal, they'd given her a lovely bouquet of flowers and box of truffles from Mouse's. Those two things alone had made her day. But now, as everyone relaxed in the family room—Noah, Andrew and Matt on the couch, Jude and Daniel on the love seat—it was time for Clint and her to make their presentation.

Clint sat on the edge of his recliner, smiling, looking like the healthy rancher she was used to seeing. "You boys might remember how your mama always liked to give you one sentimental Christmas present."

"Like the Bibles with our names engraved on the front," said Noah.

His brothers nodded.

"And those hand-painted signs with our names and the meanings," said Jude.

More nodding.

"Your mother had one more gift planned for you boys." He looked at each of his sons. "Though she never got to finish them." He cleared his throat. "Matter of fact, I'd forgotten all about them until Carly came across the box in Mona's craft room. She agreed to pick up where your mama left off so you could have them."

Carly found herself blinking away tears as she cut through the packing tape with Clint's pocketknife. "Come help me, Megan."

After lifting the flaps, Carly pulled out the red, blue, yellow, green and orange bags one by one, each color a reminder for her of which brother's scrapbook was inside.

She handed her daughter the red one. "Give this to

Noah." Then she grabbed the blue one for Andrew and the yellow one for Matt and presented them.

Megan returned for the orange one. "Whose is this?"

"That's Daniel's." She took hold of the green bag. "And this is for you, Jude." She returned to Clint's side. "You can open them now."

Colorful tissue paper flew through the air until each of the brothers had pulled out his scrapbook. When they opened the front covers, the first things they saw were the handwritten notes their mother had penned especially for them.

As she'd expected, tears fell from each man's eyes as they read her final words.

Finally, after a long silence, Noah said, "That's our mama." He sniffed, tucking his note back into the envelope. "Always trying to make us cry." He glanced heavenward. "I hope you're happy, Mama. We're blubbering like babies."

That caused them all to laugh.

Over the next few hours, they shared laughter and memories as each man went through his scrapbook. Carly couldn't remember the last time she'd cried so much.

"Would anyone care for some more cookies?" Still wiping her eyes, she brought the plastic container from the kitchen.

"Oh, no you don't." Andrew intercepted her, taking the container and passing it off to Noah. "We're not done in here yet."

Not done?

"I have something I'd like to say."

"Oh. Sorry." Heat rose to her cheeks. "Didn't mean to steal your thunder."

He took hold of her hand. "On behalf of my brothers,

I want to thank you for completing these scrapbooks for us. It means a lot to us. You mean a lot to us. Especially to me."

Boy, if she thought her cheeks were warm before, the look in Andrew's eyes had them downright flaming.

"Carly, when I'm with you, life makes more sense. You're my best friend and the love of my life." Letting go of her hand, he dropped to one knee and pulled something from his pocket.

Oh, my. He was going to...

Her heart felt as though it might burst with anticipation as he opened the black velvet box and held it out to her.

"Carly Wagner, will you marry me?"

"Um..." She held up a finger. "Hold on one second." She turned toward Megan, who was standing beside Clint. "What do you think, sweetie?"

As if her daughter's smile wasn't enough, she shot Carly two thumbs-up. "Go for it, Mom."

Unable to contain her own smile, Carly looked down at the man before her. The one she loved beyond question and couldn't wait to spend the rest of her life with. "Would you mind repeating the question?"

"You're really going to make me work for this, aren't you?"

"You ain't seen nothin' yet," said Noah.

Everyone laughed.

Again, Andrew looked up at her, his brown eyes alight with love. "Will you please do me the honor of becoming my wife, Carly?"

"Yes!"

He slipped the ring on her finger so quickly she didn't even have a chance to see what it looked like before he took her in his arms and kissed her.

She didn't care, though. She had the rest of her life to

do that. With God's help, they had finally put their pasts behind them and allowed Him to open their eyes to the future He had planned for them. A future they would now share together.

And she couldn't think of anything better.

* * * * *

If you enjoyed THEIR RANCH REUNION,
be sure to check out these other wonderful tales by
author Mindy Obenhaus:

THE DOCTOR'S FAMILY REUNION
RESCUING THE TEXAN'S HEART
A FATHER'S SECOND CHANCE
FALLING FOR THE HOMETOWN HERO

Available now from Love Inspired!

Find more great reads at www.LoveInspired.com

Dear Reader,

Life is littered with the unexpected. Yet sometimes, those events turn out to be unexpected blessings.

Andrew and Carly were a couple of misguided souls allowing their pasts to dictate their futures. They were content in their lives—they had dreams and aspirations— yet God had so much more in store for them. Things they never imagined.

I love how God works. We're going along on our merry way, doing our own thing, and then He sends us on a little detour that can change our lives forever.

I hope you enjoyed Andrew and Carly's story. I love reunion stories, and theirs was one steeped in past hurts, perceived failures and regret. Yet God used those things to draw them together and open their eyes to the truth.

And how about meeting the rest of the Stephens men? Definitely some heroes in the making.

Of course, I was thrilled to take you back to Ouray, albeit in a little different way. While the city of Ouray is nestled in a bowl, surrounded by thirteen-thousand- foot peaks, a short drive north of town and the mountains are pushed back, leaving beautiful rangeland dotted with ranches, all bordered by the majestic San Juan Mountains.

Until next time, I would love to hear from you. You can contact me via my website, mindyobenhaus.com, or you can snail-mail me c/o Love Inspired Books, 195 Broad- way, 24th Floor, New York, NY 10007.

See you next time,
Mindy

SECOND CHANCE AMISH BRIDE
Brides of Lost Creek • by Marta Perry

Widower Caleb King is set on raising his two small children without assistance from anyone—especially a relative of the wife who'd abandoned them. When Caleb is injured, Jessie Miller is just as determined to help her late cousin's family—never imagining that coming into their lives would lead to her own happily-ever-after.

THE TEXAS RANCHER'S NEW FAMILY
Blue Thorn Ranch • by Allie Pleiter

Wanting a better life for his daughter, horse trainer Cooper Pine moves to the small Texas town of Martins Gap. But he doesn't count on his daughter becoming a matchmaker! Once little Sophie decides she wants neighbor Tess Buckton as her new mommy, it isn't long before Cooper starts to see Tess as his future wife.

HIS SECRET ALASKAN HEIRESS
Alaskan Grooms • by Belle Calhoune

When private investigator Noah Catalano is hired to spy on waitress Sophie Miller, he has no idea he's about to fall for his assignment—or that Sophie is actually an heiress. Will the possibility of a future together shatter when their secrets are exposed?

HER HILL COUNTRY COWBOY • by Myra Johnson

In taking the housekeeper job at a guest ranch, all former social worker Christina Hunter wants is a quiet place to recover from her car accident. What she gets is a too-attractive single-dad cowboy, his two adorable children and a chance at the life she's always dreamed of.

THE BACHELOR'S UNEXPECTED FAMILY
by Lisa Carter

Suddenly guardian to his teenage niece, crop duster Canyon Collier is thankful to have single mom Kristina Montgomery living next door. The former Coast Guard pilot never expected that while bonding over their teens and giving the beautiful widow flying lessons, he'd begin to envision them as a family.

HEALING HIS WIDOWED HEART • by Annie Hemby

Doctor Lexie Campbell planned to spend a quiet summer volunteering at a free health clinic—until forest fires force her to move. Her days become anything but calm living next door to hunky firefighter Mason Benfield—to whom she's soon losing her heart.

Get 2 Free Books,

Plus 2 Free Gifts—
just for trying the Reader Service!

Love Inspired®

Caleb darted a quick look at Jessie, and then his gaze dropped. "You never told me about your business out in Ohio."

It took a moment for Jessie to process the unexpected words. Finally she shrugged. "There didn't seem to be a reason to."

"Or an opportunity?"

She shook her head slightly, but it was probably true. They hadn't had many casual conversations, and she tended to pick her words carefully with him.

"Zeb told me about it. He said you gave it up to come and help us."

"I couldn't be there and here, could I? It seemed more important to be here."

"Why?" His eyes met hers, challenging. "Why was this important to you?"

Jessie hesitated. She glanced at the *kinder*, but they didn't seem to be paying any attention to the adults' conversation. "I grew up being responsible for my cousin. I guess I still feel responsible. If I can do something to right a wrong, then I want to do it. I need to do it."

Jessie couldn't bring herself to look at his face, afraid of what she'd read there. He reached out suddenly to grab her wrist, covering her hand on the wheelchair, and her breath caught.

"You aren't…" he began.

But she wasn't to know what he might have said. Becky gave the chair a big shove. "We can take it the rest of the way. We don't need any help."

Jessie let go and watched the children struggle to get the chair into the barn. She wanted to assist, but not at the cost of upsetting Becky.

What had brought on that sudden reaction on the child's part? The fact that Caleb had been momentarily occupied with Jessie? She wasn't sure. But each time she took a step forward with Becky, it seemed to be followed by a plunge backward.

As for where she stood with Caleb… She didn't even want to think about that problem.

Don't miss
SECOND CHANCE AMISH BRIDE
by Marta Perry, available September 2017 wherever
Love Inspired® books and ebooks are sold.

www.LoveInspired.com

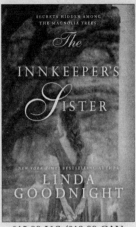

Earn points from all your Harlequin book purchases from wherever you shop.

Turn your points into *FREE BOOKS* of your choice
OR
EXCLUSIVE GIFTS from your favorite authors or series.

Join for FREE today at
www.HarlequinMyRewards.com.

Harlequin My Rewards is a free program (no fees) without any commitments or obligations.